THIS MAN'S MAGIC

How could she get her career off the
ground if no one knew her name? Sorrel
Valentine knew there was one way—if
her father would acknowledge her as his
daughter to Lucas Amory, head of
Amoroso. It was a lot to ask, but Sorrel
had never taken into account the possibility that Lucas would believe her hard-
won letter of introduction was a
forgery . . .

THIS MAN'S MAGIC

BY
STEPHANIE WYATT

MILLS & BOON LIMITED
ETON HOUSE   18–24 PARADISE ROAD
RICHMOND   SURREY TW9 ISR

*First published in Great Britain 1987
by Mills & Boon Limited*

© Stephanie Wyatt 1987

*Australian copyright 1987
Philippine copyright 1987
This edition 1987*

ISBN 0 263 75759 5

*Set in Monotype Times 10.4 on 10.4 pt.
01-0887-57423*

*Typeset in Great Britain by
Associated Publishing Services
Printed and bound in Great Britain by
Collins, Glasgow*

CHAPTER ONE

THEY were good, certainly her best work to date. But dammit, what was she going to do with them? Perched on the sofa, long legs drawn up so her chin rested on her knees, Sorrel Valentine brooded over the designs spread before her on the low table.

For five years, ever since she had left the Birmingham School of Jewellery at the end of her three-year course, she had worked steadily to build up a career, and up to a point she had done reasonably well. She had her contract to supply a set of designs four times a year for a firm of costume jewellery manufacturers, and a shop in Shepherd's Market was beginning to sell her hand-crafted pieces of fine jewellery quite regularly. But she'd had few interesting commissions as yet. It was a case of the chicken and the egg. How could the rich and famous commission work from her if they'd never heard of her? And how were they going to hear of her if no one bought her work and talked about it to their friends?

Sorrel sighed. Having cherished her independence for the last five years, she was beginning to wonder if she hadn't been *too* independent. But then, she thought wryly, no one had ever offered their help. Or perhaps she just hadn't been hungry enough. Though no one among her friends at the craft centre knew it, she could be living on the proceeds of her godmother's legacy without doing a stroke of work. Considerations other than monetary ones drove her: the need to do something constructive with her time, to use the God-given talent and the skills she had acquired at college.

Even that, if she was honest, was only part of it.

The ambition to become a craft jeweller had been born when she was twelve, after Fred Mullins had taken her around Valentine & Co, introducing her to the staff, who showed her, and allowed her to handle, some of the precious gems her father dealt in. As an adult she had come to recognise that that adolescent ambition had been an attempt to have something in common with her father who hardly seemed aware of her existence, an attempt to make him notice her and think well of her. And she was perceptive enough to realise that even now her burning ambition was fuelled by a desire to show her parents that the world thought something of her, even if they didn't.

Sherry-brown eyes gleamed with self-mockery as a bright 'Cooee . . . ' broke in on her introspection and a familiar tousled mop of marmalade-coloured hair appeared at the opening into her hall.

'Oh, you *are* here. It was so quiet I wondered . . . Charlie's starving and guess what? I've forgotten to buy bread again.' Tammy's uninhibited laughter rang out. 'I don't suppose you could . . . '

It was a familiar request and Sorrel grinned, unwinding her long legs to stand up. Tammy was always forgetting something, bread . . . milk . . . 'I've got a better idea,' she said. 'Call Charlie over and eat with me. There's a steak and kidney pie that only needs a few minutes in the microwave.'

The rest of Tammy followed the marmalade head into the room, a large lady, as tall as Sorrel herself but built on much more generous lines, her ample curves swathed in one of the swirling caftans she favoured, as brightly coloured as the stained glass she worked in. 'You're sure we won't be interrupting?' she demurred, but not very convincingly.

'At the moment, any interruption is welcome,' Sorrel said ruefully. 'Maybe you and Charlie can come up with an answer to my problem.'

'The difficult we solve at once, the impossible takes a little longer,' Tammy grinned, backing to yell across the stairwell, 'Charlieee,' as Sorrel made her way to the kitchen.

'A dockland warehouse!' her mother had exclaimed in horror when, on leaving college, Sorrel had told her she had found the place where she wanted to set up her business. But as soon as Sorrel had seen it she had known it was for her. Not only did it have spacious living accommodation with an ever-changing view of the river and a workshop unit on the ground floor, it also offered her the chance to belong to a tight-knit community of craftsmen.

Sorrel's desire to find a place for herself in a world that till then seemed to have no place for her had made her stick to her guns, and her mother had capitulated, not even taking the trouble to view the property herself. And neither had her father visited her, merely assuring her that Valentine & Co would supply her with any precious stones she wanted.

It had been her godmother's legacy that had provided her working capital and the means of furnishing her home. Originally one enormous, high-ceilinged room, it now had a kitchen and a bathroom divided off at one end. Between these two rooms was her front door and entrance hall, while above them her gallery bedroom was reached by a spiral staircase.

For the first few weeks of her occupation she had literally camped out in the vast, echoing space, owning only a bed and an easy chair. Five years had seen a lot of changes, and Sorrel had a home not even her mother could disparage, had she cared to visit. Rugs were scattered on the gleaming floor of her sitting-room. Sea-green curtains, at present closed against the dank February night, hung at the three floor-to-ceiling windows overlooking the Thames, while the collection of easy chairs and sofas were upholstered in a deeper, toning sea-green. The dining-table and six chairs, the two occasional tables and the old Welsh dresser she had picked up at a sale had been lovingly stripped down and repolished by a local craftsman, who had also built bookshelves to run the entire length of one wall with space for her stereo and collection of LPs and tapes. Her gallery bedroom was carpeted in pale apricot to match the colour-washed walls, while a burnt orange cover on her bed provided a splash of colour.

Her kitchen was well equipped too, for, having one of her own for the first time, Sorrel had discovered she enjoyed cooking. Taking one of her steak and kidney pies out of the freezer, she popped it into the microwave oven before splitting a long French loaf, spreading it with garlic butter and wrapping it in tin foil to heat when the pie was done.

As she hurried out of the kitchen to set the table, she collided with Charlie. A man in his late forties, his wild, once brown hair and beard grizzled now; a giant of a man, his head only just clearing the balcony to her bedroom, wide-shouldered and barrel-chested, his sweatshirt fighting a losing battle to meet his belted jeans over his swelling paunch. Muscular arms and hands like hams made him look more like a prize fighter than anyone's idea of an artist, and his nose reinforced that impression. Broken more than once in his eventful life, it gave him a truly villainous appearance, an appearance totally belied by a pair of bright blue eyes that brimmed over with humour.

' 'Ello, darlin'. Tam persuaded you to feed us again, 'as she?' The big cockney swept her up in his arms so her feet dangled six inches from the floor.

'Put her down, Charlie,' Tammy scolded. 'You don't maul the cook until *after* we've eaten.'

With firm ground beneath her feet and breath in her lungs again, Sorrel was able to say, 'You know where the beer is, Charlie. And if you'd open a bottle of wine for Tammy and me . . .'

With a beer can in one hand and an opened bottle of wine in the other, Charlie wandered across to sit beside Tammy on the sofa. They were still there, so absorbed in Sorrel's designs that they didn't even notice when she put the steaming, fragrant pie on the table.

They were the nearest she'd ever come to having really close friends, she thought affectionately. Both warm-hearted, tolerant people, Tammy about ten years Charlie's junior, playing the role of mother as often as that of lover. And yet the partnership seemed to work, to an extent Sorrel often found herself envying. But then she herself had never had any flair for personal relationships.

Telling herself not to get maudlin, Sorrel called, 'Come and get it,' plunging her knife into the pie's crust.

Charlie leapt up with alacrity but Tammy lingered over the exquisitely coloured jewellery designs with the specifications in Sorrel's meticulous handwriting alongside. 'These really are fabulous, Sorrel! Wouldn't this be just me, Charlie?' She brought one of the designs to the table, a necklace made up of linked scrolls of gold with a centre pendant, a large, gleaming peridot set in another scroll of gold.

Charlie's blue eyes twinkled wickedly. 'I'll say it would! I'm just picturin' you wearin' it . . . an' nothin' else.'

'Lecher.' Tammy took a good-natured swipe at him, which he ducked before saying to Sorrel, 'Are these the result of all those hours you spent in the V & A?'

Sorrel nodded, helping herself to another slice of hot garlic bread. 'I really fell for that medieval jewellery. The settings are heavy by today's standards, yet the craftsmanship was superb.'

'They're copies, then?' Tammy asked curiously, and Charlie blew a raspberry of derision. 'Shows 'ow long it is since *she* took a look round a museum!'

'Not copies, Tam.' Sorrel cast a quick glance at the pages still strewn over the coffee table: pendants, earrings, hair ornaments and chaplets, bracelets, belt buckles, long strings of jade and gemstone beads set in gold and interspersed with faceted stones, double rings meant to be worn on adjoining fingers, rings whose settings were hinged to reveal a cavity inside. 'It would be impossible to make copies today. Gemstone cutting was in its infancy then, so they used the polished stones in their natural shapes, or very primitive cutting to get more lustre and a workable shape. Not at all likely to appeal to the modern woman who expects her jewellery to sparkle. No, I tried to get into the minds of those early craftsmen to imagine the kind of thing they might come up with if they'd had some of our modern techniques.'

'And succeeded,' Charlie put in.

A gratified flush coloured Sorrel's cheeks. 'Though in a few cases I have used cabochons rather than faceted stones—moonstones, opals, star stones and cat's eyes—to enhance the Gothic effect.' She thought of the blue and white moonstones she had used in an early try-out, the completed pendant which she had given to her sister as a present for Christmas, and for which she still hadn't received a thank you!

As they sat later over their coffee, Tammy asked curiously, 'So what's your problem when you have a commission like this, Sorrel?'

'They've *not* been commissioned, and that's the problem,' Sorrel grimaced.

'You're not lettin' Mellings 'ave 'em!' Charlie remonstrated.

'That'd be a wicked waste,' Tammy concurred, her pleasant features screwed into a ferocious scowl.

'My own feelings entirely, but that leaves my only other outlet, the shop in Shepherd's Market,' Sorrel sighed.

'And you couldn't afford to make all these up on

spec,' Tammy nodded sympathetically. 'The cost of
the gold alone would be prohibitive. Thank God *my*
work doesn't call for such expensive materials! What
you need,' she went on, 'is for one of the big boys to
notice you. Someone like . . . Bulgari, for instance.'

At Sorrel's derisively raised eyebrows at the mention
of the internationally famous jewellery house, she
defended, 'It's not so out of the question, not with
designs like these.'

'The snag bein' 'ow does she get an introduction to
someone like that?' Charlie returned to the basic
problem. 'It's not so much what you can do as who
you know, and Sorrel's no better than I am at culti-
vatin' people of influence.'

'And I suppose firms like Bulgari and Amoroso
have the cream of designers on call, anyway. To break
in there you really *would* need influence,' Tammy said
glumly.

Amoroso . . . The name produced an odd inward
shiver. Her father had many contacts in the jewellery
world, and one that she was very much aware of.
Over the years in the society columns she had often
seen him pictured with Lucas Amory, sometimes just
the two men together, more often with female
companions; her father with his wife and Lucas Amory
with a wide assortment of beautiful women gazing
adoringly at him. She knew the type, having suffered
at the hands of a man very like him. But Lucas Amory
was Amoroso, and it wasn't unreasonable to think her
father might be willing to give her an introduction.

'You're looking very thoughtful, Sorrel,' Charlie
said perceptively. 'Got an idea?'

How much should she tell them? she wondered. 'As
a matter of fact,' she said slowly, 'my—I do know
someone who knows Lucas Amory.'

'It has to be female,' hooted Tammy, an avid reader
of gossip columns. 'And I doubt any lady of *his*

acquaintance would be eager to bring another woman to his attention.'

'It's a man, actually.' Better not to mention the relationship that her father had always been so reluctant to acknowledge.

'In that case, what are you waiting for?' Tammy demanded archly. 'If you're sure, that is, this *man* friend will trust you within a mile of Lucas Amory. Oh, don't mind me, love,' she added at the suddenly troubled look on Sorrel's face. 'Anyway, hasn't the gorgeous Mr Amory got a regular thing going with that Italian model now? P'raps he's finished sowing his wild oats and is preparing to settle to matrimony with her.'

Sorrel made no comment. It was remembering how distant and unapproachable her father had always been that brought a frown.

'Go on,' Tammy urged. 'Why don't you ring your friend now?'

But Sorrel shook her head. Phoning her father at home wouldn't be a wise move, not when his wife might answer. 'I don't know his home number,' realising even as she said it that she didn't even know where he lived now. 'I'll call him at work tomorrow.'

'Mr Valentine will see you now.'

Taking a deep breath, Sorrel rose gracefully to her feet, ignoring the ill-concealed curiosity of the svelte, grey-haired secretary and quelling the apprehensive flutters in her stomach. She gripped the edge of the portfolio tucked beneath her arm and stepped forward, glad now of the expensive, deep-gold wool suit she had splurged on, for knowing she looked well groomed was a wonderful boost to her flagging confidence.

Eyes riveted on the tall, lean man rising to acknowledge her behind the impressive desk, Sorrel was unaware of the secretary retiring. He looked older, but of course he was, five years older than when she had seen him last. Hair that had been thinning then was almost gone now, yet the baldness still managed to lend distinction to the smoothly dispassionate features. Eyes she seemed to remember as hazel now looked grey, though that could have been a reflection of the grey suit he was wearing.

Conscious she was staring, she became aware that his scrutiny was equally searching, though there was no welcome in it. The wary eyes were the eyes of a stranger.

Well, what else had she expected? That the five years had wrought a miraculous change? They *were* strangers. Her sherry-brown eyes gleamed with amused self-mockery as she held out her hand. 'Hello, Father.'

'Sorrel.' His voice was smoothly polite, as if she was a distant acquaintance and his hand gripped hers only briefly. He invited her to be seated, adding, 'I'm pleased to see you looking well.'

The prick of resentment at this meaningless platitude was quickly hidden behind her habitual mask of cynical amusement. 'Are you, Father? Pleased to see me, I mean? I've been on the premises often enough in the last five years. Had you wanted us to meet you could have seen me then, and I wouldn't have needed to make this appointment.'

Amazingly he seemed to flinch. 'Sorrel . . . you must understand . . . '

The cool amusement in her eyes hid the pain of her growing up years, for she had never understood why, although her father had paid her school fees and supplied her with copious pocket money, he had never once visited her. She hadn't understood why, when it was his turn to have her during the holidays, she had always been taken to stay with the family of Fred Mullins, the head security guard at Valentine & Co, only seeing her father for the occasional 'treat'. Not that she had disliked staying at the Mullins's terraced house in Hammersmith. It had been more of a home to her than the crumbling mansion her mother had moved into on her second marriage. Fred Mullins had been more of a father to her than the man looking at her so uncomfortably now, the Mullins's son and daughter more family than her own half-brother and half-sister at Thorley Hall, and they certainly meant more to her than her father's two sons whom she had never been privileged to meet.

She watched his mouth tighten into a thin line. He was going to refuse her request, she was sure of it, and her stomach churned with disappointment. And then she thought, dammit! It wasn't too much to ask.

'Father . . . ' she leaned forward, an unconscious plea in the lines of her slim body. 'I've been careful not to bother you for five years, but I need to beg a favour of you.'

The Hatton Garden traffic four floors below sounded loud in the sudden silence. At last he looked up. 'If it's within my power . . . '

'Oh, it is . . . ' Eagerness animated Sorrel's delicately chiselled features, lending a genuine sparkle to her brown eyes. 'I have some designs that would be perfect for Amoroso to produce, but if I just walk in off the street with them, the chances are no one of any importance would even get to see them. But Lucas Amory is a friend of yours, isn't he? So if you could arrange a meeting where you could introduce me, I might be able to persuade him to take a look . . . '

Her voice trailed away as she saw her father shift uneasily in his chair. 'But why Amoroso? They're top of the market with their own design team. I doubt Luc Amory ever takes work from outsiders.'

'Well, at least take a look at them yourself.' Hastily she undid the ties on her portfolio and tipped the contents out on the desk. 'If you say they're not good enough to make my name as a designer . . . '

She held her breath, watching for clues in her

father's expression as he slowly examined one sheet after another, her heart sinking as the level brows, so much like her own, drew together in a frown.

Felix Valentine's frowning gaze slid over the tall, slender girl sitting so tensely on the other side of the desk. Russet hair, slightly more red than his own had once been, wide mouth and strongly marked brows that put him in mind of his own mother in her heyday. Similar look about the sherry-brown eyes too, except his mother's eyes had never looked at him with quite such cynical fatalism as his daughter's did now.

His daughter . . . It had hit him between the eyes when she had walked into his office with the bearing of a young queen. God, but it wasn't right that they should be strangers! A surge of unaccustomed guilt and regret made his hand clench. She was a daughter any man might be proud of, beautiful, spirited, and—his gaze raked over her remarkable designs —very talented. He had really had no idea . . . And that was another indictment of his performance as a father. But there was Marcia . . .

'You say Mr Amory doesn't take work from outside designers, but what about Simon Smylik?' Sorrel demanded when the silence went on and on. 'Amoroso took him up and made his name. And that's just the boost *I* need, if I'm going to get anywhere in my career.'

Her father spoke at last. 'You have ambition, then?'

It was the first remotely personal question she could ever remember him asking, and its slightly accusing tone made her flush defensively and rush into ill-considered speech. 'Of course. I've never been any good at personal relationships, so what else do I have but my work?' The hard, searching gaze he subjected her to put her even more on the defensive. 'You don't think Amoroso would be interested in these designs, then?' she said flatly.

'On the contrary.' The words seemed to be forced

out reluctantly. 'I think Luc might well be very interested indeed.'

His surprising admission made her heart leap, only to plunge again when he went on, 'Unfortunately your request puts me in an awkward position.'

'I don't see why . . . ' Sorrel persisted. Having wrung that admission out of him she was reluctant to let the advantage go.

'Because Luc Amory is a *family* friend, not only my friend but Marcia's too. It could be . . . complicated.'

'You mean your wife wouldn't like to have me introduced as your daughter to a friend who has never heard of my existence.' Sorrel enlarged on his inference.

From her father's pained expression she gathered that he didn't care to hear the truth voiced so unequivocally. 'You mustn't blame her, Sorrel. I hurt her very badly.' As if impelled by an inner force he pushed himself to his feet and walked to the window to stare blindly into the street. 'Did your mother never tell you? How we came to marry, I mean?'

Sorrel shook her head. 'She rarely, if ever, mentions you.' It struck her that for the first time in her life, she and her father were actually talking to each other.

'But she must have spoken to you about her family background?' he began remotely.

Sorrel cleared the huskiness blocking her throat. 'Er . . . no.' And then because the bald denial seemed to need some explanation, 'You see, she's always been so wrapped up in her new family and we've never . . . talked.'

It was a bleak little admission that left so much unsaid, but even so it destroyed the comfortable illusions of the man standing at the window. He had always assumed the daughter he had abandoned on his divorce had found a secure niche in her mother's new family. 'Sir Charles—your stepfather—he was unkind to you?'

'Oh, no.' Sorrel shook her head. 'There were times when he was quite sympathetic. But you must know I lived with Ellie for three years after you and Mother split up. I was nine by the time I met Sir Charles, and they had Julia by then. They were a family and I didn't . . . belong.'

Regrets, guilt Felix had buried for nearly half a lifetime suddenly surfaced. Caught between the devil and the deep blue sea, between the wife he loved and the daughter he had wronged. He hated the idea of exposing himself, but if he told Sorrel the truth, maybe she would understand why he couldn't . . .

'Your mother's parents were . . . aristocrats,' he began slowly, keeping his back turned because what he was about to reveal couldn't be done under the cynical contempt of his daughter's gaze. 'Not titled, but definitely out of the top drawer, and poor as church mice. The house had been in the family for generations, an abbey, no less, and about as comfortable, falling about their ears. Certainly no money for the upkeep of the property or to pay staff. Which was why they attempted to clean out the lake themselves.

'By some freak accident they were both drowned, leaving Elizabeth at eighteen with a barn of a house and a mountain of debts. The only family assets were some rather fabulous jewels, rubies, which rumour had it were a gift to a Forrester ancestor from an Indian prince. The setting was entirely unsuitable as a piece of jewellery for an upper crust English lady, but the rubies were flawless. They had to be sold—along with the abbey—to pay off the debts, and I was sent down there for a preliminary viewing.'

Sorrel was listening, enthralled. These were her grandparents he was talking about, these . . . aristocrats who had met such an unlikely end. She found herself curious about this ancestral home, this abbey: where it was, who owned it now. And for the first time she realised why her mother had settled so easily into her life at Thorley after the divorce. For the first six years of Sorrel's life they had lived in London, and she had taken it for granted her mother was a Londoner. Now with this new knowledge came the realisation that her mother had merely returned to the kind of life she had been bred for.

'She was very pretty at eighteen, your mother.' Her father's voice had lost that chilling remoteness. 'Grief-stricken of course, fair and fragile and totally unfitted for the burdens she was carrying. I wasn't much older myself. She needed a strong man to depend on, and I saw myself as that man. What began as an attempt to comfort her led to . . . greater intimacy. For a few weeks she made me feel ten feet tall. I suppose I was flattered that such an upper-crust young woman should turn to me. Oh, the Valentines had money, but not a fraction of the pedigree.

'She was so damned helpless!' There was a note of anger in his voice now. And then he sighed. 'It was all too easy to mistake compassion for something deeper . . . more lasting. It wasn't until she told me she was pregnant that I began to come to my senses.'

He turned back to the room then, one hand held out towards Sorrel in an unconscious plea. 'My world, my life, my work was in London, while all Elizabeth knew were country pursuits; riding—oh yes, the roof might be leaking but there were always horses in the stables—gardening, looking after the tenants on what was left of the estate . . . My infatuation ended in seconds, but my responsibility for the results had only just begun.' He strode across the room and opened a section of panelling to reveal a well stocked drinks cupboard. Pouring a generous shot of whisky into a glass he took a long swallow.

'So you married her,' Sorrel said softly.

He turned back to her, traces of an old despair showing in his face. 'What else could I do? What had begun as a clumsy attempt to lighten Elizabeth's burdens had only added to them. I couldn't abandon her, however much my father ranted and my mother wept. And Marcia . . . God, when I remember what it was like, telling the girl I loved—and who loved me—that I was marrying someone else!'

Being of a compassionate nature herself, Sorrel could easily imagine his dilemma, and found herself not only feeling closer to her remote father than she had ever thought possible, but almost liking him. 'Yes, it's little wonder that Marcia couldn't stand the sight of me.'

Her father sighed heavily. 'You and Marcia were the innocent victims of the situation, but you both got hurt most of all.'

'And all for a marriage that had little chance of succeeding anyway,' Sorrel said wryly. 'Why didn't you just . . . pay Mother off?'

Felix swallowed the rest of his drink. 'My father wanted to do just that. But even with money it would have been like casting a child adrift. Elizabeth was so . . . dependent. And for a few months—until after you were born—it seemed to be working well enough,' he went on, staring down into his glass. 'She was busy decorating the house, preparing a nursery. And I saw nothing of Marcia. She was hurt, angry, proud, and she was avoiding me. But after the novelty of having a baby wore off, Elizabeth began to get bored, holed up in London. She missed not being able to ride. My mother had always been able to amuse herself shopping and socialising, but the people we knew . . . Elizabeth complained she had nothing in common with them. As of course, she didn't. The chasm of different life-styles, different cultures just got wider, and when there was no love to bridge it . . . And then Marcia couldn't avoid me for ever, not when her father and mine were partners.'

'I didn't know that!' Sorrel put in.

'No, I don't suppose you did,' he sighed. 'Well, seeing Marcia again only brought home to me just what I'd thrown away. And I have to admit she deliberately needled and upset your mother. Perhaps if she hadn't, Elizabeth would have agreed to a divorce much sooner. But she was jealous of Marcia. Unhappy herself, I suppose she didn't see why Marcia should be happy at her expense. Anyway, we were stuck with it, and my God, it was a cat and dog life! I don't suppose you remember . . . '

'Oh yes, I remember.' Little more than a baby and mostly in the charge of a nanny, she could still remember the bitter quarrels, the even more bitter silences.

'And then Elizabeth went to stay with some old friends in the country, and met Berisford-Reid, and after only a few weeks was not only willing but eager for a divorce.' Twenty years later the relief was evident.

'So you both married much more suitable partners, and neither had room in your lives for me.' Sorrel's matter-of-fact statement disguised that though she could now understand why, the knowledge still had power to hurt.

'I'm sorry.' Her father's usually pale cheeks carried two discs of colour. 'I thought you'd be happier with your mother. You were only six, after all.'

The cool mockery in her eyes seemed to remind him that Elizabeth hadn't wanted her either. 'I did intend having you to stay with us in your school holidays, but Marcia . . . ' His expression was almost shee-pish. 'She might have forgiven me my lapse but she could never quite forget. I *had* betrayed her after all, made us both suffer six years of misery through my juvenile infatuation, and you were a visible reminder.'

He twirled his glass between his long fingers, not looking at her. 'And still are,' he added in a voice that pleaded for her understanding. 'If I do as you ask . . .'

'She's going to have to acknowledge publicly that you have a child who has a claim on you equal to her sons,' Sorrel finished for him heavily. 'So I'm not to get my introduction to Lucas Amory.' She stood up and began to gather up her designs. The disappointment was acute, not just that he was denying her the chance to boost her career, but that she, his only daughter, was still such a negligible consideration.

'I'm sorry, Sorrel.' A hand covered one of hers. 'Believe me, I'd be proud to proclaim you as my daughter, but you must see I can't do that to Marcia against her wishes.'

Tears pricked behind her eyes and she looked down to blink them away, her gaze falling on her father's hand still resting on her own. Funny, but she couldn't remember him touching her before.

'Yes. Thank you for telling me,' she said when she felt she could trust her voice. But she had allowed her façade of amused tolerance to slip and the pain was there in her eyes for her father to see.

'I'd still like to help you,' he said impulsively. 'It would have been some time, anyway, before I could have arranged a meeting with Luc. Marcia and I are off on holiday to Barbados tomorrow. But what if I wrote you a letter of introduction?'

Sorrel's spirits began cautiously to rise. 'You'd do that?'

Her father crossed to the drinks cabinet again, poured a shot of brandy into an empty glass, and without asking if she wanted it, thrust in into her hands. 'I'll go and see my secretary. Drink that while you wait.'

Sorrel thought over the things her father had told her. His account had carried the ring of truth: two people, very young, making all too human mistakes until they were caught up in events they couldn't control. He had been right, though, the two innocent victims—herself and Marcia—were the ones to suffer most.

She was surprised to find her glass was empty by the time her father came back from the outer office. He was carrying a letter in an unsealed envelope which he took out and handed to her.

It was quite brief, introducing her to his friend as someone whose work would be of great interest to him. Just one line riveted her attention. She lifted her eyes, wide and vulnerable, to her father's face. 'You—you've acknowledged me as your daughter,' she whispered. 'I didn't expect . . . '

His mouth twisted wryly and there was a ghost of a smile in his eyes, making them appear warmer. 'I think I can rely on Luc to be discreet.'

'Thank you.' For an awful moment Sorrel was afraid she would burst into tears. Instead she impulsively kissed her father's cheek, and was rewarded with an awkward pat on the shoulder. 'If you like,' she offered huskily, 'when I see Mr Amory, I'll ask him to be sure he never mentions my name in Marcia's hearing.'

Her father nodded, the twist of his mouth even more wry. 'And Sorrel, when you come here to buy stones in the future, have them tell me. I find myself, belatedly, wanting to get to know my daughter.'

Sorrel fought the lump in her throat. 'And I you,' she whispered.

When she reached the street she was still clutching the letter in her hand as if it was something precious. As it was, because written there for the recipient to see was 'My daughter, Sorrel Valentine'.

She was not to know the trouble that recognition was to cause her, nor the direction from which that trouble was to come.

CHAPTER TWO

THERE was no time like the present, Sorrel told herself. It was already Friday afternoon and if she waited until she got home to telephone for an appointment, it would probably be well into next week before she would get to see Lucas Amory. Her feet hardly feeling the ground beneath her feet, she walked the two hundred yards down Hatton Garden to the Amoroso building.

It took persistence to get past the stolid doorman but, if the highly decorative blonde secretary was everything she had expected of a man with Lucas Amory's reputation with the ladies, at least she tried to be helpful.

'I'm afraid Mr Amory won't be in again today,' she revealed when Sorrel had stated her name and business. 'But as it's a design matter, perhaps you should see Miss Killingley first. She's the head of our design team.'

It wasn't what she wanted, but Sorrel felt she could hardly refuse, and allowed the secretary to take her along the corridor to another office and introduce her.

If Lucas Amory had chosen his secretary for her looks rather than her ability, that couldn't have been the case with Miss Killingley, a thin, overstrained little woman in her forties. Before Sorrel could open her mouth she was saying wearily, 'Oh, not another one! Miss Valentine, Amoroso *never* buys outside designers' work.'

As she had done with her father, Sorrel questioned, 'Never, Miss Killingley? What about Simon Smylik?'

only to be rewarded by a further tightening of the rat-trap mouth.

'And ever since, we've been *inundated* with hopefuls like you, trying to find an easy way to the top.'

Sorrel decided she didn't like the obstructive woman one bit, but held on to her temper. 'Never *easy, surely,*' she returned. 'And I do come well recommended.' She indicated the letter of introduction lying on the desk between them. 'I really think you should at least give Mr Amory the chance of reading that and making up his own mind.'

The woman reached out a disdainful hand and a moment later was slitting open the envelope. Conscious of the confidential nature of what the letter revealed, Sorrel protested, 'Hey! That's addressed to Mr Amory!' only to be ignored.

But at least what she read brought Miss Killingley to a more conciliatory attitude. After a searching glance at Sorrel she said grudgingly, 'OK, I suppose it won't do any harm for me to take a look.' Without asking permission she opened the portfolio and started thumbing through the pages, betraying nothing of her reaction beyond a worrying of her bottom lip with her teeth. When she had studied the last one, she again picked up the letter of introduction and re-read it.

'All right, Miss Valentine,' she said at last. 'If you'll leave all this with me, I'll bring them to Mr Amory's notice.'

'Oh, but——' For some reason Sorrel didn't feel happy about this proposal. 'I will be able to see him? I can make an appointment?'

Miss Killingley's thin mouth curled contemptuously and Sorrel could almost see her thinking that here was yet another female hoping to catch the roving eye of her employer. 'If he thinks it necessary, Miss Valentine.'

An angry flush stained Sorrel's cheeks, but she could hardly insist that she wouldn't have the slightest interest in meeting Lucas Amory had it not been for the possibility of Amoroso using her designs. She cast another glance at them lying on the desk and rose reluctantly to her feet. 'Very well, Miss Killingley, but hadn't you better write down my telephone number?'

More than once over that long, anticlimactic weekend, Sorrel wondered if the sour-faced Miss Killingley would succeed in blocking her approach to Lucas Amory as Sorrel suspected she would like to, but at half past ten on the Monday morning, as she was repairing a bracelet in her workshop, the phone rang.

'Miss Valentine? This is Mr Amory's secretary. Mr Amory would like to see you this afternoon at two-thirty, if that's convenient.'

'Yes. Yes, that's fine. Thank you very much.' Sorrel put the phone down, her heart banging against her ribs, palms suddenly slippery with perspiration. Wiping them against her stained jeans, she knew they would never be steady enough to carry on with the intricate work she had been engaged in when the phone call had interrupted, and anyway, she *had* to tell someone. Charlie was out on one of his perpetual sorties of London with his sketch-book, but Tammy should be in her workshop. Dropping the bracelet into a velvet-lined box and locking it into a drawer, she carefully returned her tools to the rack before hurrying across to her friend's unit.

'He's asked to see me, Tam,' she burst out, her voice shaking with excitement. 'Lucas Amory. He wants to see me this afternoon!'

'That's great, Sorrel!' Tammy straightened up from the large table cluttered with fragments of brightly coloured glass and strips of lead. If Charlie had to struggle to make any money from his painting, Tammy's stained glass work was in great demand, some of it already installed in venues as varied as a cathedral, the conservatory in a minor stately home and a London gaming club. 'But then I knew he would, once he'd seen those designs of yours, and your friend's introduction would make sure of that.'

Out of consideration for her father, Sorrel had still not revealed to her friends her relationship to the man who had supplied that all-important introduction.

'You're home and dry, darling,' Tammy crowed. 'Now, what are you going to wear?'

Sorrel burst out laughing. 'A raincoat, of course. Have you looked outside today?' 'February fill dyke' was living up to its name; the rain had been slashing down all morning swelling the grey, turgid river that swept past the building. 'Does it matter? I'm hoping to interest Lucas Amory in my designs, not give him designs on me!' Then at the expression on her face she promised quickly, 'It's all right, I'll change into a clean pair of jeans.'

'You will not!' Tammy declared forthrightly. 'And of course it matters. Oh, I know it's your designs he'll be buying, but if you're going right to the top, you're going to have to promote yourself. Sorrel Valentine, designer *extraordinaire!* Come on, let's take a look at your wardrobe.'

Calling to Kit, the glass engraver who had the adjoining workshop, that they would be in Sorrel's apartment if either of them were wanted, Tammy hustled her out through the rear door and up the three flights of stairs.

'You wouldn't have any of your delicious quiche going begging, would you?' Tammy asked hopefully flopping down to recover her breath on one of the long sofas. Smiling, Sorrel cut her a slice and added it to the coffee tray she was preparing. 'Well, it *is* nearly lunchtime,' Tammy excused herself as Sorrel put the tray on the table between them. 'Aren't you having any?'

'You're kidding! The way the butterflies in my stomach are behaving right now?' Sorrel grimaced.

Tammy licked the last crumbs from her fingers. 'Oh, darling, he's only a man.'

'Huh?'

'Lucas Amory. That's who you've got butterflies about, isn't it? I'll give you a tip, love. Every time you find yourself feeling in awe of him think of him paring his toenails.'

Sorrel gave a muffled snort of laughter.

'And it it's some haughty bitch being snotty with me, I imagine her——' Tammy broke off, grinning. 'No, perhaps I shouldn't sully your innocent ears with that one. What have you got to be nervous about, anyway? Lucas Amory's the lucky one to be getting the offer of your designs, and don't you forget it, my girl. Come on now, let's decide what you're wearing. What about that silk suit I bullied you into buying from Solly Green?' Solly was one of her numerous friends, an East End clothing manufacturer who supplied West End boutiques charging three or four times the price he could be beaten down to by a resourceful Tammy. 'I've never seen you wearing it yet.'

'Because I've never found the right occasion,' Sorrel retorted, leading the way up the spiral staircase. 'And if you haven't noticed, it's still raining cats and dogs out there.'

'So?' Tammy opened the wardrobe and riffled among the hangers until she found what she was looking for, the matt black, heavy silk skirt and jacket. 'You have an umbrella, don't you? And you'll take a taxi door to door. Oh, yes you will . . . ' she added threateningly as Sorrel was about to protest. 'If you can't afford it, I'll pay for it myself. First impressions count.'

It was like being swept along by a tornado. 'All right,' Sorrel found herself acquiescing weakly. 'Though I pay for my own cab.' It always gave her an uncomfortable feeling whenever Tammy and

Charlie assumed she was as hard up as they were. Would they think differently about her if they knew she was actually a wealthy woman? It wasn't a question she'd ever dared put to the test.

Tammy took over, sweeping down to the kitchen to press the suit while Sorrel had a bath, blowdrying her freshly washed hair into a riot of gleaming russet curls falling to her shoulders, and bullying her into rather heavier make-up than she usually preferred, and Sorrel went along with it with tolerant amusement. Only when she was being helped into the black silk jacket that went with the hip-hugging skirt slit to the knee did she begin to have misgivings.

'Tammy, I *can't* wear this without a blouse underneath. It's not decent!'

'And ruin the effect?' Tammy was scandalised. 'Of course it's decent—just.' She had done up two of the buttons that cinched the jacket in at the waist, leaving the top one undone to reveal a lot of cleavage and the soft swell of the upper part of Sorrel's creamy breasts. 'If you've got it—flaunt it,' Tammy grinned, wielding the perfume spray and enveloping Sorrel in a cloud of Balmain's Ivoire. 'It's a marvellous background for your wares.'

She clasped on the necklace and bangle worked in two shades of gold and handed the matching ear-rings to Sorrel to fix herself, jewellery borrowed from stock, for, as Tammy insisted with irrefutable logic, 'Today you're a walking showcase for your designs and craftsmanship'

A walking showcase for *something,* Sorrel thought, surveying her mirror image with incredulity.

'My God! With your figure you look good in an old sack, but I never realised till now you're one very sexy lady!'

Tammy's comment echoed Sorrel's unease. What with the slit in her clinging skirt and the button of the jacket left undone, she felt dangerously exposed.

Ignoring Tammy's anguished protests, she firmly did up the remaining button.

Her appearance still bothered her, as if she was dressed up inside someone else's skin as she stepped from the minicab outside the Amoroso offices. But rather comfortingly the doorman was still just as stolid when this time she was able to tell him she had an appointment, nor did the blonde secretary raise so much as an eyebrow when she told Sorrel Mr Amory hadn't got back from lunch yet and invited her to take a seat.

Here was none of the old world graciousness of her father's office. Lucas Amory went in for modernity: a grey mixture wall-to-wall carpet, pearl-grey walls and the sleek, uncluttered lines of Scandinavian furniture. And of course there were photographs—covering the whole of one wall—of some of the world's most beautiful women displaying Amoroso jewellery.

There was plenty of time—a full fifteen minutes—for Sorrel to take stock of her surroundings before the outer door opened. But the first person to walk through was female, quite the loveliest girl Sorrel had ever seen, jet-black hair falling around a piquant, high cheekboned face with a flawless olive complexion, the corners of the red-lipped mouth still upturned in a smile that was echoed in the slumberous dark eyes.

Sorrel recognised at once the Italian model, Bianca Fratelli, but it was the man who followed her in, his arm protectively around her shoulders, who drew irresistibly Sorrel's gaze. Dark and dangerous was her instant impression. Dark jacket fitting superbly across broad shoulders, dark trousers encasing long legs. Dark hair as black as night against the silver wings at his temples, black eyebrows and lashes framing black, indolently gleaming eyes, and all thrown into relief by a teak-tanned skin. Younger looking than those silver wings in the hair suggested, not strictly handsome taken feature by feature; high, wide cheekbones, a forceful chin, lines slashing from a rather beaky nose to a beautifully chiselled mouth as he smiled down at the girl at his side.

The photographs she had seen had shown a good-looking man, but they had not shown his almost visible aura of male sexuality, and it struck Sorrel now like a blow in the solar plexus.

Ignoring her as they walked in, she had time to think how alike they were, both with their dark, Italianate looks. They might almost have been brother and sister—or father and daughter, for the young model couldn't be more than eighteen or nineteen.

And then those black eyes were fixed on Sorrel herself, with none of the indolent pleasure with which he had been regarding his companion. An inward shiver ran through her, and she found herself on her feet with no recollection of how she got there.

'Ah! Miss . . . Valentine?' His voice was deep and gravelly. 'I'm so sorry to keep you waiting.'

It was a politely conventional apology, but offered with such a blatant lack of sincerity that Sorrel's hackles rose, though she gave no sign of it as, safe behind her defensive mask she returned smoothly, 'That's quite all right. It was good of you to see me, Mr Amory.'

'I hope you continue to think so, Miss . . . Valentine.' His second hesitation over her name was somehow un-nerving, but nowhere near as un-nerving as the open sexual appraisal he was now subjecting her to, his dark eyes sweeping over her from the top of her russet head to her slender ankles and narrow feet, lingering speculatively over her rounded hips and what she still felt was too much exposed of her breasts. Colour burned in her cheeks, and she cursed herself for letting Tammy talk her into wearing this outfit, wishing she was safely encased in the wool suit she had worn for the interview with her father.

'Very nice, but I'm afraid the goods on display are

not going to tempt me to overlook your deception, as I'm sure you were counting on,' he drawled derisively, both his tone and the direction of his gaze telling her he wasn't referring to her jewellery designs.

Sorrel stared at him blankly, several emotions conflicting for supremacy; shock at the bizarre direction this interview had taken, outrage that he seemed to think she had engineered it in order to meet him, to offer herself as a candidate for his bed, embarrassment that he should have made such an insulting inference in front of his girlfriend and his secretary, bewilderment at his reference to her deception.

Bewilderment superseded the rest. 'Deception, Mr Amory? I have no idea what you mean.'

'Do you not?' Sorrel had had no idea until that moment that dark eyes could look so cold and wintry. 'I'm referring to your forgery, of course. You didn't really think you'd get away with it, did you?'

'*Forgery!*' She was beginning to think she had been given the wrong scenario. Either that or she was having a nightmare and would wake up in a minute. 'You surely don't think I've copied my designs from someone else?'

'We're talking about the letter, as you very well know,' Lucas Amory said coldly. 'Your so-called letter of introduction. An excellent forgery, I have to admit, and I'd love to know how you did it——'

'But it *isn't* a forgery,' Sorrel broke in indignantly 'I was there when my father——'

'Your father!' he sneered. 'My dear Miss . . . Valentine—if that indeed *is* your name—if you'd done your research a little more thoroughly you'd know Felix Valentine is a very close friend of mine. I've known him for fifteen years or more, and his family, too.' He stepped closer, looming over her threateningly. 'Felix Valentine has two sons, boys I know very well. *Sons,* Miss Whoever-you-are. He has no daughter.'

Sorrel closed her eyes. It just hadn't occurred to her
that Lucas Amory would disbelieve her father's letter,
and she doubted it had occurred to her father, either.
So what should she do? She was tempted to tell him
the full story, but she was only too aware there would
be witnesses to the revelations she knew her father
would prefer not to be disclosed, the openly curious
secretary and the slightly more sympathetic-looking
model.

'Look, if you'd just telephone my father, he'll tell
you——' she said desperately, and when Lucas Amory
merely looked even more sardonic, she turned to the
secretary. 'Please, just get my—Mr Valentine on the
phone.'

'Most convincing, Mystery Lady,' the hateful man
mocked. 'I really do have to admire your nerve. But
then you picked your time, didn't you? You must be
aware that Felix Valentine is out of the country just
now'

And would be for another four weeks, Sorrel thought
with despair, only now remembering her father
mentioning his forthcoming holiday in Barbados. 'Yes,
I'd forgotten . . . ' How could she possibly convince
him now that she was telling the truth? For a few
moments her thought processes seemed to seize up,
and then she remembered that there *was* one other
person who knew about the letter and its contents.
'My father's secretary!' she exclaimed. 'He dictated it
to her. *She* will tell you it's genuine.'

But this disclosure didn't have the hoped for effect.
While the secretary looked uncertainly at her employer,
he merely grinned wolfishly. 'But surely you know
Mrs Oliphant always takes her holiday at the same
time as your 'father'?'

Sorrel's shoulders slumped as her last chance of
proving the truth of her claim disappeared. So much
for her hopes of her father's letter proving an 'open
sesame'! She had been right in the past to value her

independence. Relying on other people put you in their power, laid you open to humiliation and hurt. Well, it was a lesson well learned. She would rely solely on her own efforts in future, even if it took her whole lifetime to get where she wanted.

'Well, if that's all you got me here for, Mr Amory, to accuse me of imposture . . . ' She drew away from him, turning blindly towards the door.

'Not so fast, Mystery Lady.' He gripped her shoulder to detain her. 'I have to remind you that forgery is a criminal offence. I think I should hand you over to the police.'

It was the touch of his hand rather than his threat to call the police that finally brought her temper boiling over. Logic told her she couldn't really blame Lucas Amory for suspecting her story, not when he had known her father's family for so many years without hearing a whisper about any daughter. But he was playing with her like a cat with a mouse, positively enjoying her humiliation and impotence, and she *hated* him for that.

Turning, bringing her arm up sharply, she threw off his hand. 'Yes, you *do* that, Mr Amory, as long as you don't mind finishing up looking a fool. And if my father forgives you for dragging his name into the newspapers, I doubt very much if his wife will.'

The young model suddenly crossed to his side, tugging at his arm and whispering in his ear. He frowned as he listened, then straightened, still looking sceptical. 'Miss Fratelli suggests you might be telling the truth and that there might be a good reason why you're never mentioned in Mr Valentine's family circle. That you are, in fact, Felix's illegitimate child?'

Sorrel saw genuine sympathy in the girl's dark eyes, but Lucas Amory merely looked watchful, as if waiting to see if she would snatch at this way to get herself out of a tight corner. Damn this big, arrogant man who was so sure of himself, so certain he knew it all

and couldn't possibly be wrong. Damn her father for
forcing her into this false position and his wife who
couldn't forget old grievances. Damn even the pretty
model whose sympathy she hadn't asked for and
didn't want. Drawing herself up she spat, 'No, I'm no
bastard. I don't carry my birth certificate around to
prove it and I no longer care whether you believe it
or not, but I am the legitimate daughter of Felix
Alexander Valentine. Now, about my designs, Mr
Amory . . .'

For some reason that last outburst had hit Lucas
Amory where all other shafts had missed, and he
looked furiously angry. 'You surely don't imagine I
could still be interested in them, Miss Valentine,' he
bit out. 'Amoroso would never dream of doing business with such a devious, conniving little cheat.'

Her gleaming, sherry-coloured eyes mocked him but
behind her mask she winced, each insult hitting like a
stone. 'I was merely asking for the return of my
property,' she said with spurious sweetness.

'They're still with Miss Killingley, I presume,' he
said distantly.

'Thank you, you won't mind if I go and recover
them then.' Her knees were shaking, but somehow she
made it to the door, where she turned to face her
adversary again, and the air seemed to crackle with
antagonism. 'And when you do finally talk to my
father——'

'Oh, I shall certainly talk to Mr Valentine as soon
as he returns,' he broke in savagely. 'I'm sure he'll be
most interested to learn how his family is supposed to
have grown overnight, and even more interested to
discover how you managed to perpetrate your forgery.
Don't think you've got away with this.'

'Tell him,' Sorrel went on as if he hadn't interrupted, 'that I've changed my mind about offering my
designs to Amoroso. It's not a company I could ever
feel comfortable to be associated with.'

It was quite satisfying to have had the last word, but her anger dissipated quickly, and she was feeling physically sick by the time she found her way to Miss Killingley's office, only to find the door open but the room empty. She ought to go in search of the woman, she knew, but if she didn't sit down she was afraid she might pass out, so she pushed open the door and went in.

She was still breathing deeply to quell her nausea several minutes later when Miss Killingley walked in. 'What are *you* doing here?' the woman demanded suspiciously. 'I thought Mr Amory had got rid of you.' She smiled with a certain smug reminiscence. 'He didn't take at all kindly to the deceit you practiced on him.'

'I've only come to collect my designs, then Amoroso will be well rid of me,' Sorrel promised sardonically.

'Oh, yes of course.' She reached into a drawer and took out Sorrel's portfolio, asking with surprising interest, 'These designs . . . What are you going to do with them now?'

'Does it matter?' Sorrel asked wearily. And because she still felt sick and shaken by what had happened in Lucas Amory's office she added gloomily, 'Probably burn the lot.'

CHAPTER THREE

As THE road curved over the brow of the hill, the house stood silhouetted against the dusk skyline, many windows illuminated. 'There it is,' Sorrel said. 'The entrance is down in the valley on the left.'

The little van jerked as Tammy's foot lifted from the accelerator in surprise. '*That!* My God, when you said Thorley Hall I thought you meant a *village* hall, not a ruddy great mansion!' Very little fazed Tammy but for once shock, astonishment, and above all curiosity, robbed her of breath. She had known Sorrel Valentine for five years now, and until a few days ago had assumed her to have no family. To discover she not only had a mother living but that she came from a background like this . . . 'What in hell are you doing living in *Wapping* when you have a home like this?' she demanded, even more curious to see Sorrel's face suddenly wiped clean of expression.

Sorrel wondered if she was going to regret having asked Tammy to come tonight. More, if she was going to regret having accepted her mother's surprising invitation at all. This charity ball was the social highlight of the surrounding district and Sorrel had never been asked before, but this year, not only had a pressing invitation been extended, but her mother had suggested Sorrel brought with her a collection of her jewellery to display.

It wasn't as much as she had hoped for from her father nearly six weeks before, but since Lucas Amory had dashed all hope of advancement from Amoroso, the chance of *any* showcase for her work was welcome,

36

even if it meant a large slice of her profits would go to the charity.

Thinking of Lucas Amory and his accusations could still make her squirm, and she wondered if her father had talked to him and put him straight yet. If he had, there had certainly been no apology from Mr Amory. Not that she wanted one; the thought of seeing him again gave her the shudders.

Tammy and Charlie had been surprised and very indignant on her behalf when she had told them merely that Lucas Amory had turned down her designs. They had encouraged her to try other outlets, but Lucas Amory's savage rebuff had knocked her self-confidence for six and she was only just beginning to climb out of her depression when her mother's telephone call had come. And as Tammy had been with her at the time, and her mother hadn't considered how she was to get to Thorley, she had taken up her friend's offer of transport.

'My mother's home, Tammy, never mine,' she said quietly. 'I only spent part of my school holidays here.' She suppressed a shiver, for some of the most desolate times of her childhood had been spent at Thorley.

But Sorrel refused to think of that now, and as Tammy slid the van into a parking space on the gravel sweep, she said, 'Come on, let's get unloaded.'

They lifted out the suitcase containing the dresses they would change into and the showcases of jewellery, and Sorrel led the way through the massive front entrance into the high, echoing, empty hall. It was like stepping back into her childhood, overwhelming her with the knowledge that she didn't belong.

It was the ebullient Tammy's 'Wow!' that recalled her to the present, and she told herself wryly that she should be used to her lack of welcome at Thorley by now. The sharp tap of heels had her turning towards the doorway to the ballroom to see a dark-haired woman wearing a shrimp-pink evening dress and a harassed expression appear.

'About time, too!' she exploded on seeing them.

Sorrel stared at her in astonishment. 'I beg your pardon?'

'You are the jewellery, aren't you?' the woman demanded impatiently. 'You're in the Painted Salon.' Indicating they were to follow, she turned back into the ballroom, missing the startled glances Sorrel and Tammy exchanged.

The sound of feminine chatter reached them before they stepped through the door at the far end into a smaller room with a high, painted ceiling that had been jewel-bright once but that was now faded and peeling, where they found half a dozen stalls had been set up and were being decked out with craftwork ranging from wood-carving to lace-making.

'Lady Berisford-Reid said this one was to be reserved for the jewellery.' The woman halted beside the one remaining stall. 'As you can imagine, there's been some resentment about it being reserved. Those who got here first couldn't see why it shouldn't be first come, first served.'

'Your mother's a *lady*? Does that make your step-father a lord?' Tammy sounded so overawed that Sorrel grinned.

'No love, only a baronet. He's a sir, not a lord.'

A strangled gurgle from the woman in shrimp-pink recalled her attention. 'You're Lady Berisford-Reid's *daughter?*' she croaked. The poor woman looked as if she expected to be consigned to the dungeons for her gaffe. 'Should I let her know you've arrived?'

'Perhaps if you could find me a cloth to cover this trestle, and a couple of chairs?' Sorrel suggested.

'Yes . . . yes of course . . . only too pleased.' She scuttled off and Tammy fell about laughing.

'*That* made her change her tune,' she gurgled. 'Self-important old bat. I'll get this lot set out when

Dracula's wife gets back. You go and say hello to your Mum.'

Grinning her thanks, Sorrel retraced her steps through the ballroom where a man was setting out small chairs on a dais for the musicians, crossed the echoing hall and began to mount the curving staircase. Rapping firmly on the door of the master bedroom leading directly off the gallery, she listened, and at an irritated, 'Who is it?' went in.

The room was large, so large that not even the dark, heavily carved furniture diminished its proportions, certainly too large for the antiquated heating system to make much impression. Every bit as shabby as Sorrel remembered, threadbare patches in the Turkish carpet, wooden shutters holding back the night at the tall windows, because to have released the heavy red curtains from their golden cords would risk damage to the rotting fabric.

Her mother sat at the dressing-table, a petite woman in her middle forties, blonde hair fading now, bare, plump shoulders rising from the ice-blue satin of her evening gown, the diamonds in their ornately old-fashioned setting that had been in the Berisford-Reid family since the days when they had wealth to go with their social position scintillating against her white skin.

'Sorrel!' Pale blue eyes stared at her daughter as if she was the last person she had expected to see. 'What's the matter? Hasn't that Angela Millwall shown you where to go?'

'Good evening, Mother. And it's lovely to see you, too!' Sorrel's gentle mouth twisted ironically. How long since she and her mother had last met? Six months? Nine? And that, only a hurriedly shared tea at Richoux in Piccadilly.

Her mother flushed as she crossed the room and reached up to peck her eldest daughter's cheek. 'I'm sorry you think my manners are lacking but there's been so much to see to . . . '

Nothing had changed. It had always been her mother's constant theme, so busy, so much to do that was of more importance than the daughter whose existence was a reminder of a mistake she would rather forget. Sorrel sighed, breaking in, 'Apart from wishing to say hello to you, I need to know whether my friend and I are invited to dine with the family or take our sandwiches with the staff.' She hadn't meant to phrase the question so bluntly but the disappointing lack of welcome removed any conscience about putting her mother on the spot.

'It never occurred to me you'd want to dine with us.' Her mother turned back to the mirror, her colour even more heightened. 'You've never shown an inclination for our company before.'

Sorrel flinched at the injustice of this accusation. 'Perhaps because I've never been invited, Mother.'

Feeling herself on the defensive, Elizabeth Berisford-Reid's hands stilled as she reached for her ear-rings. 'Since when do you need an invitation to come home? Your room's always ready for you.'

Except that this had never been her home and Sorrel had never spent any time in it except at an express invitation. 'So I'm to eat with the staff,' she said flatly.

'If you'd given me some warning . . . ' Elizabeth irritably fixed diamond clips to her ears. 'You young people . . . no consideration. Why, it was as late as this afternoon when Julia told me she'd asked a boyfriend from London to stay. If *you* insist on upsetting my table arrangements as well . . . I do so hate making people sit elbow to elbow.'

So even her sister's boyfriend took precedence over herself, Sorrel thought bleakly. 'Don't worry, I wouldn't dream of upsetting your arrangements.' She lifted her chin, refusing to show how wounded she was.

There was a hard, painful lump in her throat that threatened to turn to tears as she left her mother's room. Knowing she couldn't return downstairs until she had got herself together, she turned blindly for the passage leading to the room she had always occupied at Thorley, praying she wouldn't bump into her young half-sister who had the larger room opposite. The corridor remained empty and, reaching the desired haven, she pushed open the door, her hand reaching for the light switch.

But the light was already on and, though the room was empty, there was evidence of occupation—a suit-case open on the bed, masculine hairbrushes lying on the dressing-table. So much for her mother's assertion that her room was always ready for her, she thought bitterly, closing the door and retreating down the corridor. At a guess this was where Julia had installed her boyfriend, which left the problem of where she and Tammy were to change.

They managed in one of the downstairs cloakrooms, after they had set out her display of hand-crafted jewellery which included a few of the smaller items she had made up from the 'medieval' range Lucas Amory had turned down. But although her mask of cynical amusement had been firmly back in place by the time she had returned downstairs, the hurt was there in the painful tightness of her chest and throat.

It was still there three hours later when the music drifting in from the ballroom rose to a crescendo, and after a drum roll, the voice of the bandleader announced the supper interval. 'Didn't they say they'd bring refreshments to us in here?' Tammy asked.

'Yes, but I could do with something stronger than coffee,' Sorrel said feelingly. 'You hold the fort here while I fight my way to the bar.'

'Good thinking.' The flamboyant Tammy flopped into one of the chairs. 'I could murder a pint.'

Sorrel followed the departing crowd, tall, slender, unafraid to add extra inches to her height with spiky-heeled gold sandals. She had considered her own ankle-length brown velvet skirt and pin-tucked cream silk shirt quite elegant when she had set out, but compared to the elaborate ball gowns the other women wore she felt like a common sparrow trying to compete with birds of paradise.

Moving with unconscious grace she was skirting a group blocking the doorway into the stone-flagged hall when a hand fastened on her arm. 'Sorrel, I've been looking for you,' her mother hissed.

Allowing herself to be drawn aside, Sorrel's eyebrows rose. 'I wouldn't have thought I'd be difficult to find. This is the first time I've left my post all evening.'

If the irony in her voice was noticed, it was ignored. Her mother's pale eyes flickered over her eldest daughter's understated outfit, registering disapproval. 'Surely you could have worn something more suitable, Sorrel. A lot of people here tonight know we're related, and it's not as if you have to watch your pennies like we do. I don't know what they must think . . .'

The intricately fashioned gold hoops in Sorrel's ears swung as she stiffened defensively. 'That I'm here to work, of course.' Her retort was tart, but retaliation had never gained her her mother's approval and wouldn't now. 'Anyway, you're elegant enough for both of us,' she managed lightly. 'If you were looking for me to find out how your charity's going to do out of me this evening, I don't think you'll be disappointed.'

Her mother stared at her blankly, then frowned. 'No! No, it wasn't that. Something much more important.' She drew Sorrel further out into the hall. 'You live in London, so you must be able to tell me something about this man Julia's brought home. A Lucas Amory?'

Sorrel was so staggered she could only gape. Lucas Amory, here at Thorley? How ironic! She had expected to be able to meet him through her father, not her mother. If only she'd waited they would have avoided all that stupid misunderstanding over her father's letter. Not that it would make any difference now. She certainly didn't intend to cross his path again.

'Well? Do you know him?' Her mother broke into her chaotic thoughts.

Sorrel pulled herself together. 'I've met him,' she said shortly, thinking of the queue there would be at the bar and wishing herself miles away from this inquisition. 'He owns Amoroso Jewellery, though I believe he has numerous other interests. Has quite a thing going with that Italian model, Bianca Fratelli, according to gossip, and they were together when we met. It doesn't seem to stop him getting between the sheets with any woman who's willing, though.'

At her mother's gasp, Sorrel's eyes widened. 'Did you say *Julia* brought him? How on earth did she meet him?'

'You might well ask!' Anxiety etched a furrow between her mother's fair brows. 'She was so set on going up to town to get a new dress for tonight, so I let her stay with a schoolfriend. I can only suppose she met him then. When she said she'd invited someone down, I naturally assumed it was a boy her own age. You can imagine how I felt when I met him at dinner, especially as Julia seems besotted.'

From that, Sorrel deduced that Julia had turned a deaf ear to any motherly warnings. Something twisted painfully inside her breast. Her mother had neither known nor cared whom Sorrel had been associating with at Julia's age. Pushing aside her own feelings she said with a frown, 'I can understand Julia losing her head over him, but why would he accept her invitation? He must be twenty years older than she is.'

'Far too old for her, even without his unsavoury reputation,' her mother agreed. 'Can't *you* talk to her, Sorrel?'

She gave a breathy, incredulous laugh. 'Mother, since when has Julia ever listened to me?'

'Perhaps if you'd cared for her . . . but you were always too wrapped up in your father's family to have any time for mine.'

The injustice of this accusation took Sorrel's breath away, but she knew better than to argue, protecting her vulnerable feelings behind a mask of derision.

Her mother's truculence subsided and there was a gleam of speculation in the blue eyes she turned on Sorrel. 'It's a pity you didn't trouble to dress up, and I can't say I care for the impression you give of laughing at us all, but I dare say a man like Lucas Amory might find it intriguing. You're not as pretty as Julia, but you *are* nearer the man's age.'

Sorrel gasped aloud as she followed her mother's tortuous train of thought. 'You're not suggesting I try to cut Julia out with this man! Oh no, Mother. I don't like him and the antipathy was mutual.'

She might as well have saved her breath. 'It would have been better if you had been at dinner,' her mother pressed on. 'But I'll bring him to the Painted Salon after the interval.' And before Sorrel could raise another protest she was gone.

The interval was over and the dancing had resumed by the time Sorrel had secured their drinks. The fun waxing faster in the ballroom had almost emptied the smaller salon where the stalls were housed when Tammy suddenly gasped, 'My God! Isn't that Lucas Amory? Sorrel, now you'll be able to have another stab at interesting him in your designs.'

With a sick lurch of her stomach, Sorrel closed her eyes and muttered, 'Oh *hell!*'

Certain the malevolent fates were about to deal her another dirty hand, because having to meet Lucas Amory again was bad enough without having him insult and humiliate her in front of her mother, Sorrel turned slowly and felt a measure of relief that there were only two people strolling towards her.

As golden-blonde as their mother had been in her

youth, Julia had piled her hair high in a sophisticated style. That, and the slinky sapphire-blue jersey gown that revealed more of her precociously voluptuous curves than was decent, made her look older than her years.

But as her gaze flickered to the man at her sister's side, her heart suddenly slammed against her ribs. He was even more darkly attractive than she remembered from that one traumatic meeting. No wonder her little sister had been swept off her feet. He had a charisma a girl as young and inexperienced as Julia could have no possible defence against. A hard lump of anger settled in Sorrel's chest. Bianca Fratelli hadn't been more than nineteen, now he was turning his attentions to her sister who was still only seventeen. Were his sexual appetites so jaded he needed nubile young girls to titillate them? She was surprised how forcefully she hated that idea. Well, there was nothing she could do about Bianca Fratelli, but she'd certainly frustrate his intentions concerning Julia or she'd die in the attempt.

But none of her turbulent thoughts were visible on her face as the couple stopped in front of her, neither did she flinch when that hateful voice said silkily,

'Well, there's a thing! You do manage to pop up in the most unlikely places, Miss . . . Valentine.'

Sorrel lifted her chin and stared him right in the eyes. 'On the contrary, Mr Amory, I believe it's you who is out of place tonight.'

Julia looked like an actress who'd just had her best lines stolen. 'Do you two know each other, then?' she demanded jealously.

'No, we don't know each other at all.' Sorrel flicked him a dismissive glance and then ignored him. 'Hello, Julia.' Her deceptively lazy gaze noticed the necklace she had given her sister for Christmas and the way it drew the eyes to the girl's voluptuous curves, and it occurred to her this man might have no idea how young Julia really was. Taking a deep breath she went on deliberately, 'You're looking very grown up tonight, love.'

As she expected, her sister's sapphire-blue eyes flashed furiously at the patronising comment. 'And you're looking even more of a dried-up old spinster,' Julia retorted spitefully.

Lucas Amory's eyebrows climbed in surprise. 'Is this a private fight or can anyone join in?' he queried.

Sorrel's chuckle brought his head swinging back to her, his eyes narrowing. 'Strictly family.' The lazy amusement in her eyes mocked him. 'Julia hasn't learned yet that it's not done to keep it up in front of strangers.'

The further allusion to her youth had Julia's colour high. 'Oh, but you're not a stranger, are you, Luc?' she said quickly in a transparent attempt to recover her surface veneer of sophistication. 'Anyway, I didn't come to quarrel with you, Sorrel, but to look at your jewellery.'

Sorrel watched resignedly as her sister noticed the other prototypes of her 'medieval' range of designs, pouncing at once on the ear-rings that matched her necklace. 'You admired my pendant, Luc, so what about these?'

'Let me see.' He took them from her reluctant grasp and examined them closely before relinquishing them again to Julia's avid hands. Slanting a strangely searing glance at Sorrel he demanded, 'You make all your own jewellery?'

'Of course.' Sorrel lifted her chin proudly, wondering if he recognised them from the designs she had submitted to him.

Tammy thought it was time she entered the lists on her friend's behalf. 'Sorrel's a first class craftswoman, but she's an even more brilliant designer,' she said in a 'put that in your pipe and smoke it' tone.

He raised a sardonic eyebrow but before he could

comment Julia was asking excitedly, 'I can have them, Luc?'

Sorrel stiffened, gasping, 'Julia! You can't allow a man you've only just met to buy you expensive jewellery!'

Julia's blue eyes were stormy, her bottom lip jutting. 'Don't be so stuffy, Sorrel. You're too old-fashioned to be true.'

'I don't think so.' Sorrel was aware that Tammy was becoming almost apoplectic to see her not only turning down a sale but uncaring if she offended the man she had been so keen to please only a few weeks ago. 'What are you planning to do with them? Hide them away and wear them on the sly, or make it obvious to your parents you're prepared to sell your favours?'

Her sister blushed scarlet with mortification but insisted defensively, 'I don't see it's any of your business.'

'I'm inclined to agree,' Lucas Amory broke in with cutting sarcasm. 'Or do you question the morals of all your customers before you sell?'

Sorrel was a tall girl, in her high heels only a couple of inches short of six feet, but she still had to fling up her head to face him squarely. 'Only when my sister's involved,' she challenged, feeling a kind of satisfaction at his astonishment as Julia disclaimed, '*Half*-sister.'

'Don't split hairs.' Sorrel rounded on her, too disturbed to save her sister's feelings. 'I know for a fact Mother would be horrified if you allowed this man to buy you jewellery, a man old enough to be your father.'

She heard his sharply indrawn breath with a feeling of exultation. Let him wince! To ram home the truth she went on, 'If you want those ear-rings, Julia, you can have them. It's your eighteenth birthday in a few weeks so they can be your present from me.'

That Julia *had* lied about her age was apparent now

her secret was out. Her eyes spat fury before turning
a look of appeal at Luc. But neither were aware of
her. Sorrel was staring in challenging contempt at the
man whose hand was gripping her arm, while he
answered her challenge with a gleam of devilish
mockery. 'While Julia makes up her mind which
bauble she wants, you and I can argue over who pays
while we dance.' His dark eyes held an expression that
sent a shiver down Sorrel's spine.

But before she could claim she couldn't leave the
stall, Tammy was urging, 'Yes, go on, Sorrel. I'll hold
the fort here.' And Tammy thought she was doing her
a favour, Sorrel thought gloomily as, his hand like a
manacle round her wrist, Lucas Amory drew her
away.

They reached the edge of the dance-floor and, not
taking his eyes from the frozen defiance of her face,
he pulled her into his arms. Expecting him to return
to the argument over who should pay for Julia's
present, she was thrown into utter confusion when he
remarked, 'Didn't I see you sneaking out of my
bedroom earlier? What were you after?'

There could only be one bedroom he was referring
to, and wild colour flared in her cheeks until she told
herself firmly she had no cause to be embarrassed.
Lifting her chin she said coolly, 'I wasn't sneaking. I
was expecting to be able to change there as that has
always been *my* room. The guest rooms are on the
other side of the house.'

'This gets better and better.' The darkly mocking
eyes raked over her face and slid lower to the unbut-
toned neckline of her silk shirt, and lower still to the
firm breasts clearly outlined by the soft fabric. 'Does
that mean we shall have the pleasure of sharing it
tonight?'

She was aware the outrageous question was meant
to bait her and refused to rise to it. 'Whoever shares
your room, it won't be me. I never intended staying

the night, even though——' there was a bitter twist to her soft mouth '——only moments before my mother had been assuring me my room was always ready for me.'

He dropped his flirtatious manner. 'Perhaps she didn't know I'd been given that room. It was your sister who had it in hand.'

And Sorrel knew why Julia had chosen it, because it was close to her own. 'Ah yes, my foolish little sister. I should think she's chosen her birthday present by now, don't you?'

'Probably.' He had been holding her loosely as they danced but now he pulled her against him, one hand at the base of her spine, the other holding hers captive against his chest. 'It won't hurt her to wait.'

'You're wasting your time,' Sorrel warned him.

'Oh, I don't think so.' His dark glance moved over her face speculatively, the arm at her back drawing her closer still until she was very much aware of his hard, muscled body.

It wasn't the kind of smothering clinch she had sometimes had to fight off from men who'd had too much to drink, and she couldn't say she found his proximity repulsive. All the same, every nerve in her body tensed and she had to force herself to relax. 'I do,' she said quietly. 'You've lost the argument over who pays for Julia's ear-rings before you've begun. I only have to refuse to take your money.'

'You could, but you won't,' he said confidently. 'Because I promise you, the price of those ear-rings are *all* you're going to get out of me.' His hand tightened on hers painfully. 'Was that plot to get into my office your way of restoring the family fortunes?'

'There was, and is, no plot,' Sorrel asserted angrily.

'Oh, come on, you can drop the fiction of Felix Valentine being your father now I've run you down to your lair.'

'You haven't spoken to him, then?' She felt a shaft

of disappointment. It would be very satisfying to watch this man having to eat his words.

'We haven't had occasion to meet since he came home. And in fact I'd forgotten the incident until I found you here tonight.' He sounded bored. 'I was following up something I thought was entirely separate, though now the pieces of the jigsaw are beginning to fit.'

'Ah yes, chasing my little sister.' Sorrel saw the opportunity to return to their original argument and grabbed it. 'I don't doubt you're a very experienced man, Mr Amory, but I'd rather you reserved that experience for models and society butterflies and didn't practice it on my sister.'

'Especially as I'm old enough to be her father?' There was an edge to his voice and Sorrel knew that shot had gone home.

'Well, aren't you?' she challenged.

'As she turns out to be only seventeen, yes.' There was a wry quirk to his mouth and the concession was made reluctantly. 'Not old enough to be *your* father, though.' He examined her face, at the same time insolently moving his left hand against her breast.

Sorrel hoped he hadn't noticed her suddenly indrawn breath. 'Maybe not, but if you're egotistical enough to imagine I'm trying to prise my sister from your clutches on my own account, then think again.' She firmly moved his hand away before delivering cuttingly, 'It's my mother who's worrying about the undesirable man Julia dragged home.'

She felt him stiffen, saw the leap of incredulity in his eyes and heard it in his voice. 'Undesirable!'

'Wouldn't you say so? You're what—forty?' She knew that was exaggerating and as she inspected his face as thoroughly as he'd inspected hers moments before, she had to admit that in spite of the silver wings in his hair, he looked younger than the thirty-six the newspaper columns reported him to be. 'More than twice Julia's age, and with a reputation for womanising that would hardly endear you to her parents.'

'But rich.' His voice didn't betray it but he was angry, his sudden crushing grip telling her so.

'Not rich enough for them to turn a blind eye to your attempts to seduce their daughter,' she returned smartly. 'Because that's the object of the exercise, isn't it? I can't imagine marriage, let alone with a child bride, is quite your scene. And even if it was, my mother is the last person to find a man acceptable just because he's wealthy.'

'That I doubt, but you're right about marriage.' The bone-crushing grip on her hand relaxed and she was able to flex it cautiously. 'Why limit myself to one green apple when there's a whole orchard of juicy peaches waiting to fall into my hand?' His grin was derisive and cruel.

Sorrel was amazed at herself. Not normally so outspoken, she had been blunt beyond the point of rudeness with this man. His attitude to women in general and his designs on her sister in particular earned her unqualified distaste and she was glad if she had made him angry, yet she found this verbal sparring with him exhilarating.

'And you still think warning Julia off is going to thwart my evil intent?' he asked cynically.

'No, but then I told Mother that was useless.' Unconsciously she sighed. 'And I know it's no use appealing to your finer instincts.'

'I should say not, because I don't have any, at least where women are concerned.' The music was romantic, the movement of his body against hers slow and languorous. 'You could try appealing to my baser instincts.'

Sorrel looked up questioningly, trying to fight the spell those movements were casting over her. 'Mr Amory——'

'The name's Lucas. Luc to my intimate friends. Go on, say it.'

'Very well.' Her lips twitched up at the corners. 'Would you mind explaining what you're getting at . . . Lucas?'

'Not at all, Sorrel.' His voice was silky smooth and seductive. 'As you're so anxious to save your little sister from my evil clutches, I'm suggesting you can achieve that by offering yourself in her place.'

CHAPTER FOUR

ALL TRACE of Sorrel's habitual cynically amused expression was wiped away as her eyes widened in shock to meet the oddly cold amusement in his. 'In your bed, you mean?' she croaked.

But, of course, he wasn't serious. Only a few minutes ago he had been accusing her of being a schemer with criminal intent. She felt annoyed with herself for being momentarily taken in and covered her lapse by asking sweetly, 'You often proposition women within minutes of meeting them?'

'I don't usually have to.' His voice was warmly seductive but his eyes were watchful.

'You mean they're only too eager to crawl into your bed.' She had meant to sound contemptuous but it came out huskily because just for a few seconds she had been imagining what it would be like to be made love to by him, to surrender to his blatant sexuality, and she was horrified at herself.

Quelling the rising heat in her blood she said with a convincing pretence of boredom, 'Much as I'd like to save Julia from her youthful folly, that self-sacrificing I am not!'

'You know, Miss Berisford-Reid——'

'*Valentine,*' Sorrel snapped. 'Sir Charles is my mother's second husband.'

But he ignored her assertion. 'For a girl who's got herself into a very sticky situation, your unconciliatory behaviour is most unwise.'

The threat was unmistakable, but the band had come to the end of a set, giving her the excuse to extricate herself. She tried to walk away from him quickly but the dispersing couples impeded her and she was conscious of his hand still on her waist. 'You're still refusing to let me pay for Julia's trinket?' he asked.

'I'm still refusing,' she bit out.

'How surprising. How very surprising,' was his soft response.

Tammy looked brightly questioning when they reached the Painted Salon, but Julia complained resentfully, 'Luc, you've been ages!'

'Have you decided what you want?' he asked.

'Yes, the ear-rings of course, to match my pendant.' She looked at him appealingly. 'You are going to buy them for me, aren't you?'

He slanted a glance at Sorrel. 'Your sister won *that* argument . . . ' He paused as if to imply there were others over which she hadn't had her own way.

'Sorrel always was a prude,' Julia said sulkily.

Aware of Lucas Amory's speculative gaze on her she agreed readily, returning the ear-rings to their box and handing it to her sister.

'Didn't you forget something?' He picked up one of her business cards, studying the address on it.

'Julia knows where to find me,' she shrugged.

'But I don't.' He carefully put the card away in his wallet.

'Why should you want to?' Julia demanded jealously.

'Who knows when it might come in useful?' There was a hard implacability in his voice that sent shivers down Sorrel's spine. 'Come on, little one, let's have one last dance.' He turned Julia around, giving her a gentle push towards the ballroom. 'Goodnight, Sorrel.'

'Good*bye, Mr Amory,*' she said firmly and watched them go, hearing Julia's plaintive, 'What do you mean, one last dance? It's early yet.'

'Well?' Tammy was almost beside herself, bursting

with curiosity. 'Is he having second thoughts about your designs?'

'The subject never arose,' Sorrel evaded.

'You didn't mention it? Honestly, Sorrel, how could you waste such an opportunity?'

'As he left me in no doubt six weeks ago that my designs didn't interest him, meeting him here tonight would hardly change his mind,' Sorrel said flatly. 'I think we could pack up and go home now.'

'Sorrel, what in heaven's name have you done to Julia?' Her mother rushed up in a flurry of indignation as Sorrel was writing the cheque for the charity's share of her profits. Glad that Tammy had taken the last of the stock to the van and wouldn't witness any more family dissension, she handed the cheque to her mother who pushed it into her evening purse without even looking at it. 'Whatever it was, she's gone to bed in floods of tears and Mr Amory has decided to go back to London.'

Unable to quell a surge of gladness, Sorrel folded the borrowed cloth. 'Isn't that what you wanted, Mother? To detach her from a most unsuitable man?'

'Yes . . . ' her mother allowed grudgingly. 'But I didn't expect you to upset her so. What *did* you say to her?'

'As a matter of fact it was what I said to *him* that seems to have done the trick.' A reminiscent smile curved her mouth. 'I told him the truth, that not only was he old enough to be Julia's father but that his dubious reputation made him undesirable to her parents.'

'Sorrel, you didn't!' Elizabeth Berisford-Reid stared at her eldest daughter in horror. 'Surely not even you could be so rude to a guest in my house!'

Sorrel's throat still ached with tears she was too proud to shed as she walked quickly across the echoing hall to the front door, shrugging on her coat. What gave her mother the idea that Julia had the monopoly of feelings that could be hurt? she wondered. Stupid. *Stupid!* Self pity was an emotion she didn't admire and never allowed herself. Dashing a hand across her eyes she started down the steps, but when she reached the spot where Tammy had parked the van there was only an empty space.

A hand gripped her arm as she looked round in puzzlement and a gravelly voice said, 'It's all right, I sent your friend on ahead. We'll reach London before she does.'

There was little light out on the forecourt but Sorrel had no difficulty in recognising Lucas Amory. 'Since when would Tammy act on your instructions?' she demanded angrily. But she very well might, she realised with an inward groan. Tammy would think she was doing her a service, giving her this chance to be alone with the man who could do so much for her career.

'Since I told her *I* would be driving you home,' he said maddeningly. 'She didn't seem to think you'd have any objections.'

'Then she was mistaken,' Sorrel snapped.

'I wonder why,' he said softly, 'when you went to such lengths to meet me before. Or can I guess? You've finally realised you've got yourself in too deep and now you want to run for cover. Oh no, Mystery Lady. I take great exception to being made the victim of your criminal activities.'

He had never seemed more pantherlike, or more threatening. 'C-criminal?' Sorrel stuttered.

'Forgery, deception, misrepresentation, and, I have good reason to suspect, theft,' he listed for her astounded ears. 'So you see, there's no way I'm going to allow you to cover your tracks.'

Sorrel licked suddenly dry lips. 'Y-you're mistaken, terribly mistaken.' She thought frustratedly that just one telephone call to her father could have straightened this out, and suddenly she was angry again. 'And I'm damned if I'll go anywhere with you.'

'You know someone else who'll take you back to London tonight? If, as you claim, you have nothing to hide, where's the harm in letting me take you home?' He turned her towards a white Mercedes coupé, the passenger door standing open, and bundled her inside.

Taking the seat beside her, he leaned across to secure her safety-belt before fastening his own and switching on the ignition. The interior of the car was unashamedly luxurious but Sorrel found it impossible to relax. *Why* had he done this? Considering his attitude ever since they had met she couldn't seriously believe he was transferring his attentions from her sister to herself. Nor could she take seriously his threats concerning her supposed criminal activities, not even this last accusation of theft. It was so ludicrous he had to be bluffing.

But, having got her into his car, he seemed in no hurry to talk, beyond asking for directions to get them through the country lanes. Even when they reached the motorway he chose a tape on the cassette player rather than conversation and Sorrel, still seething at his high-handedness but with a streak of uneasiness underlying her anger, was glad to be left with her thoughts. They soon overtook Tammy's van, his powerful car eating up the miles, and when they reached London his knowledge of the East End surprised her. Only for the last quarter of a mile did she have to give him directions.

'You live *here?*' he asked as the car drew up outside the former warehouse.

Sorrel climbed out, slamming the door, and he quickly followed. 'The entrance is round the corner,' she said resignedly, having known she wouldn't get rid of him so easily.

'Got your key?' She fumbled in her bag and as soon as her fingers closed round it he removed it from her grasp, fitting it into the lock, opening the door and pushing her inside.

The light on the stairs seemed very bright and Sorrel blinked, her pulse beating very fast. 'I can manage to find my own way upstairs, thank you.' She covered that extra beat with dry flippancy.

'Oh, I always see a lady to her door,' he drawled, and she had no alternative but to follow him up the stairs, indicating the first door on the left when they came to the final landing.

She allowed him to unlock the door, then put a hand out to grasp his wrist. 'You've seen me to my door, now can I have my key back?'

'But of course.' His wrist twisted as he pressed the key into her palm, but before she could withdraw her hand he lifted it to his mouth, his black eyes watching her as he kissed it lingeringly. 'And now I want to see what's on the other side of that door.'

The sensation of his warm mouth moving sensuously against her skin shook her so much it was several seconds before she registered his words, and by then he had opened the door, found the light switch and was moving down her hallway.

'Mr Amory!' she called after him in exasperation. 'For pity's sake, it's two o'clock in the morning and I'm tired.'

But he was already moving away from her, taking no notice. By the time she had caught up he was standing in the middle of her living-room, looking round with absorbed interest.

Intent only on throwing him out, Sorrel found herself wavering. She was very proud of the home she had made for herself and not at all averse to his appreciation of it. She watched while he prowled around, taking in the details: the pleasing shape of the wrought iron standard-lamp and the coloured glass shade Tammy had made for it, the high quality modern pottery and glassware she collected, and her books, shelves of books because, when she was growing up a solitary child, books had always been her friends. He spent some time studying one of the two paintings she had of Charlie's, the one of the street market, studying it so closely that she was glad the other painting, a portrait, was safely hidden from his sight up in her gallery bedroom. Looking at that portrait always made Sorrel uncomfortable because it revealed altogether too much of her private, inner self, and to have this man sharing Charlie's perception of her would be . . . dangerous.

'Look, I really do think you should go now.' She had meant to sound positive and was horrified when the words came out on a pleading note.

And he caught it, even if he didn't bother to glance in her direction. 'Why? You did say you had nothing to hide.'

She stared at him in frowning puzzlement. 'No, I don't, but I still think this is a gross invasion of my privacy. If you like to come back in the morning and tell me——'

'And give you time to get rid of the evidence? Do you take me for a fool?'

'Evidence? Evidence of what, for heaven's sake?' she demanded in exasperation.

He had reached her desk with her drawing-board alongside and without replying began to turn over the pages of her sketch-book, sketches that Sorrel would be the first to admit were nothing special. Since he had turned down her designs six weeks ago she had been too disheartened for the creative juices to flow.

Dismissing them with a disdainful flick of the wrist, to her stunned astonishment he turned his attentions to her desk, opening the top drawer which contained her paints, closing it irritably to open the one beneath.

'Now wait a minute . . . ' Uneasiness had given way to anger at his nerve. 'You force your way into my home without invitation and now you seem to think you can go through my belongings! Just who do you think you are?'

He turned his head to look at her, his eyes flat and hard. 'Oh, I know very well who I am. The question is . . . who are you?' And while she gaped at him in impotent fury he slid open the wide, shallow drawer above the kneehole, stood for a frozen few moments then took out the portfolio she had left at Amoroso for him to see. A second later the strings were untied, and as the medieval set of designs spilled across the desk top he let out a long drawn out 'Aaah!'

'Is *that* what you were looking for?' For a couple of seconds hope leapt. 'Lucas, if you'd only asked——'

'Mr Amory to you,' he clipped, his cold voice lashing with such ferocity she gasped.

She hadn't used his first name consciously, and she was at a loss to know why he should seem so angry, but calling on her considerable reserves of pride, she drew herself up. 'Very well, *Mr Amory!* You've seen those designs before, and if you'd told me you wanted to take another——'

'Indeed I *have* seen them before,' he ground out furiously. 'Now perhaps you'll tell me what this series of Amoroso designs are doing in your possession, you little thief.'

'Amoroso designs?' Sorrel stared at him incredulously, sure she must have misheard. 'Either I'm going crazy or you are. Did I hear you claim these are *Amoroso* designs?'

'There's nothing wrong with your hearing,' he snapped.

'Then let me remind you, you turned them down six weeks ago, *Mr Amory*,' she said angrily, 'and I certainly have no recollection of you changing your mind and negotiating for them since.'

'Turned them down?' He frowned, and then his brow cleared. 'Oh I see, you're going to pretend these

are the designs you were hoping your forged letter
would get me to buy.'

Sorrel shook her head in angry bewilderment. 'I'm
not pretending anything. You know very well these
are the designs I brought to Amoroso.'

'They were apparently the designs you *left* Amoroso
with,' he ground out. 'How you worked the switch I
don't know, but by God I'll find out.'

'Switch?' It finally dawned on her what he was
accusing her of. 'You mean you're actually accusing
me of *stealing* them? My own designs? My God, you
really *are* crazy! Look, Mr Amory, these are the
designs I brought to your office. Your designer, Miss
Thingummy can corroborate that; she looked at them
in front of me. They're the ones you saw too, so
don't——'

'I didn't trouble to look at whatever designs you
brought in, not once I'd read that forged letter,' he
said in a bored voice.

'It was *not* a forgery,' Sorrel insisted between gritted
teeth.

'Oh, come on, admit you've lost this one. My design
department has been working on this range for weeks
and they're almost ready to go into production, so
you might as well confess——'

'What!' Her mind pounced on the one salient point
of his incredible claim and she was almost apoplectic
with outrage. 'You're saying Amoroso are producing
these without my permission? And you're trying to
get away with it by accusing *me* of stealing? It's not
me who's the thief, Mr Amory, it's *you!'*

'And you've missed your vocation, Miss Whoever-
you-are. You'd make a fortune writing crime fiction.'
He actually began to collect up the designs from the
desk top as if he had every right.

Furiously, Sorrel slapped the drawings out of his
hand. 'You little vixen!' Hard hands gripped her
shoulders and she knew real fear as she was shaken

unmercifully. 'I'm sick of playing games with you. It's
a pity, and had we met under more auspicious circumstances we might——' He bit off the rest of the
sentence, releasing her so suddenly she lurched against
the desk as a rough cockney voice demanded, 'What
the 'ell's goin' on 'ere?'

Lucas Amory whipped round to face the intruder,
a giant of a man who almost filled the narrow hall,
wearing only hastily dragged on jeans and still shrugging his huge frame into a shirt.

'Charlie . . . ' Seeing his familiar face in a suddenly
nightmare world had Sorrel running to throw herself
into his arms where, to her shame, she burst into
tears. 'Oh, Charlie, he—he's trying to steal my designs,'
she sobbed. 'He g-got rid of Tammy and sh-shang-
haied me. Th-then he started searching the place . . . '

'What d'you mean, 'e got rid of Tammy?' Charlie
questioned sharply, pinning the other man to the spot
with his ferocious gaze.

'He—he sent her off in the van, so I'd have to let
him bring me home.' Sorrel sniffed inelegantly and
wiped her eyes with her hand.

'But she's all right?'

'Yes, she's still on her way back.'

'All right, chick.' Charlie patted her shoulder clum-
sily. 'And 'e ain't 'urt you?'

As she shook her head the man still standing rigidly
by the desk sneered, 'Very touching. I might have
known you'd have a bully boy not too far away. I
suppose he's in on the fraud, too.' His mouth twisted
in distaste. 'Funny, I'd have credited a girl like you
with better taste.' Sorrel's colour flared at the impli-
cation that she and Charlie were lovers, but he was
going on in a hard voice, 'Not that it matters. You'll
both be in gaol before your feet touch the ground.'

It might have been expected that such a remark
would provoke a man as big and villainous-looking
as Charlie to violence but he merely asked calmly, '

'Oo is this geezer, Sorrel? Looks the type as'd 'ave the Commissioner of Police in 'is pocket.'

Sorrel's laugh was slightly hysterical. 'He probably has, Charlie. He's Lucas Amory, head of Amoroso Jewellery.'

'Is 'e now?' Charlie gave the other man a long, searching look. 'Well, I'll rearrange 'is face a bit for you if you like, but it might make more sense if we sat down an' tried to get to the bottom of this mix-up.'

Sorrel saw Lucas Amory's eyes narrow warily, and much as she would have liked to see him flat on her carpet, she had the feeling he could be handy with his fists too, and she didn't want to see Charlie hurt. 'I suppose we'd better talk,' she said wearily. 'Though trying to hold a conversation with Mr Amory is like trying to talk to the Duchess in *Alice in Wonderland* —nothing he says makes sense.'

With a gesture, Charlie indicated a chair to Sorrel's unwelcome visitor and after a momentary hesitation, Lucas Amory acquiesced, his mouth tightening grimly as Charlie took a seat between him and the door. Sorrel went back to the desk to pick up her strewn designs, choosing to sit right there to mount guard.

'Now,' Charlie said calmly. 'P'raps you'll tell me just what you're accusing Sorrel—and apparently me—of doin'.'

'It's my designs,' Sorrel rushed in. 'The ones I submitted to Amoroso six weeks ago and *he* turned down. Now he's claiming that they're his—he's putting them into production without paying me a penny! He's nothing but a crook, Charlie!'

'I don't pay extortion money to *anyone*,' Lucas Amory said grimly.

' 'Ang on, 'ang on.' Charlie brought them both to a glowering silence. 'We'll get nowhere with a slangin' match. Let the man say 'is piece first, huh?'

Sorrel subsided and Lucas flashed her a sardonic

glance, leaning back and looking perfectly relaxed while she seethed impotently. 'One Monday morning a few weeks ago, the head of my design department brought me a portfolio of unsolicited designs accompanied by a letter of introduction.'

'But a few minutes ago you said you'd never even looked at the designs,' Sorrel broke in triumphantly.

'Neither did I.' At Charlie's raised eyebrows, Lucas Amory went on to explain, 'The letter of introduction was patently a forgery, purporting to come from Felix Valentine, so of course I wasn't interested in any designs the forger had to offer.'

'But what made you think it wasn't genuine?' Charlie asked.

'Because it introduced the designer, Sorrel Valentine, as his daughter, that's why. I've known Felix for many years and he *has* no daughter, as I pointed out to your . . . friend when I summoned her to see me that same afternoon.'

Charlie, who had been frowning as he listened, looked at Sorrel. 'I thought you said it was a *friend* who could introduce you to Mr Amory.'

Sorrel saw with a sinking heart where her reticence on that point had led her. Now even Charlie was disbelieving her. 'It's a long story, Charlie,' she sighed. 'But I can assure you Felix Valentine *is* my father and that the letter was *not* a forgery. I was there in his office while he dictated it to his secretary, and he let me read it before he sealed the envelope. It——' tears pricked behind her eyes, '—it was the first time he'd publicly acknowledged me as his daughter.'

'And if you believe that, you'll believe anything,' Lucas Amory said disgustedly. 'I doubt if Valentine is her real name at all.'

'It 'as been for the five years I've known 'er,' Charlie said.

'Then if it is, she used the coincidence to "choose" Felix as a father in order to perpetrate her fraud,'

Lucas retorted nastily. 'Don't you think even if she was his bastard he'd have introduced her to me personally?'

Sorrel flinched against the hurt, because he was only echoing her own thoughts. Her father *could* have done, discreetly, without upsetting his wife. 'No one is able to choose their father, Mr Amory,' she said quietly. 'I've just been unlucky in mine.'

She saw the look of annoyance tighten his jaw but, before he could retort, Charlie was asking, 'But surely, Mr Amory, you checked on the letter with Mr Valentine?'

For just a moment Lucas Amory's supreme confidence faltered but he recovered quickly. 'Mr Valentine was away at the time, a fact Sorrel must have been aware of or she'd never have tried the trick. By the time he came home . . . frankly, I'd forgotten the incident.'

'So what brought you here tonight, claiming Sorrel has stolen your designs?' Charlie wanted to know.

Once again, absolute certainty exuding from him, Lucas told him, 'Earlier this week I was at a party where I met a young lady wearing a necklace I recognised as a design from an Amoroso range that hasn't been released yet.'

'*My* design,' Sorrel gritted.

'The young lady in question was very cagey as to how she'd come by it. She was very young and easily impressed.' His lips curled as he glanced at Sorrel's furious face. 'It wasn't difficult to angle for an invitation to a ball to be held at her family home. And what should I find when I get there? None other than my Mystery Lady. First I spotted her sneaking out of my bedroom, then later I found her presiding over a display of jewellery that included several more items from Amoroso's new range. Naturally I followed it up, sending the very co-operative friend on alone so Sorrel would have to travel with me. She was very reluctant to have me come up here, and——'

'Of course I was reluctant,' Sorrel spat. 'Any woman who knows your reputation would be reluctant to be alone with you in her apartment in the early hours of the morning.'

'You don't mean you took it seriously when I teased you about taking your sister's place in my bed?' he mocked. 'A sophisticated lady like you? Oh no, it wasn't your virtue you were concerned to keep under wraps, it was *those*. Amoroso's complete new range.'

To her horror Charlie asked curiously, 'Supposin' Sorrel did feel the need to ride on somebody else's back, 'ow do you reckon she might've managed it? Got copies of your designs, I mean?'

His words fell like stones on Sorrel's ears but Lucas Amory shrugged. 'For a lady of her resourcefulness it obviously wasn't too difficult. She visited Amoroso's premises on two occasions, and both visits she spent some time in my head designer's office.' His mouth tightened grimly. 'I'll get to the bottom of it.'

His story must sound so plausible to Charlie, Sorrel realised with a sick feeling in the pit of her stomach, especially as she'd never mentioned to him the identity of the writer of her letter of introduction. She felt horribly alone as her despairing glance fell on the disputed drawings. Was Lucas Amory really going to be able to cheat her out of the best designs she had ever done?

People, men mostly, she thought bitterly, had been doing her down for most of her life. First her father, who had shuffled her out of his life like something shameful, depriving her of her birthright, of his love and guidance. Then Max, smooth-tongued, fornicating Max, who had preyed on her need to find someone to love, who had taken her eighteen-year-old innocence and left only disillusion. Then there was Trevor, solid-seeming, conventional Trevor, who had wanted to marry her but whose love had also turned out to be counterfeit. Ironic really that Trevor should have wanted her only because he *knew* her father's identity and hoped the relationship would do much for his career, and now here was Lucas Amory, feeling free to stab her and steal her work because he *didn't* believe in the identity of her father.

Rage bubbled up inside her until she felt like a pot about to blow its lid, her fingers picking at the pages on her desk, the designs that this arrogant, pig-headed, devious man was claiming were his. *Her* designs, her babies that she'd laboured over for months, first roughing out the early ideas, then developing a couple of them and making up the prototypes to make sure her ideas would work in practice before——

Her brain slid into another gear. The prototypes! One of which she had given to her sister last Christmas. The pendant which Lucas Amory had recognised when Julia had worn it and that had been the means of tracing back to Sorrel herself. Why hadn't she thought of it before? She could *prove* her claim to the designs!

Opening her mouth to give voice to her thoughts, she bit the words back. Proving she was the legitimate owner of the designs wasn't going to be enough. What Lucas Amory had tried to do to her, stealing her work and trying to brand her a thief, had been shoddy and beneath contempt. If he could do it to her, he could do it to other unsuspecting designers. She had to nail him. If she couldn't see him committed to prison, at least she would show him up for what he was, a cheap shyster.

She became aware of Lucas watching her and realised she would have to be careful not to give the game away too soon. She wanted him to dig his grave a bit deeper yet. 'So he's convinced you I'm a liar and a cheat and a thief, Charlie,' she said, getting to her feet, and it wasn't hard to put an emotional break in her voice.

Charlie's blue eyes twinkled at her. 'I only said *supposin'* you felt the need to ride on someone else's back. I *know* you don't need to when you 'ave ideas oozin' from yer pores like sweat.'

She felt a wave of warmth towards this big, untidy man who was demonstrating his faith in both her talent and her integrity.

'Well, of course, I'd expect you to support your . . . friend,' Lucas Amory sneered offensively.

Charlie cast mildly reproving blue eyes over him. 'Better not let my Tam 'ear you makin' suggestive remarks like that, mate. Very possessive is Tam, an' very maternal towards Sorrel. Come to that . . . ' he turned to Sorrel reflectively, 'I reckon I wouldn't have done such a bad job of fatherin' you either. Better than yer own dad, anyway.'

'Oh, you would, Charlie, you would.' There were tears in her laughter as she leaned over his chair to hug him.

'Two things about this mix-up strike me,' he went on imperturbably. 'In the first place I don't know as I can see a gent in your place stoopin' to do down a struggling designer and nick 'er work. The risk wouldn't be worth the candle.'

'Charlie!' Sorrel protested. 'If he's claiming my designs as his then he's as guilty as hell.' She cast Lucas a venomous look. 'And I reckon he'd crawl on his belly, never mind stoop, if there was money in it.'

'When 'e stands to lose 'is reputation as a businessman?' Charlie questioned, and Lucas inclined his head in ironic thanks.

'Oh, he's going to do that all right,' Sorrel muttered under her breath, but Charlie was already asking, 'You say you didn't look at Sorrel's designs yourself?'

'That's right.' He glared at Sorrel. 'I've always steered clear of anything shady.'

Sorrel's temper was rising again but Charlie pursued his train of though tenaciously. 'But *somebody* must've looked at 'em, and liked 'em enough to make copies.'

'Now we *are* getting into the realms of fantasy,' Lucas said irritably. 'I can vouch for all my staff. None of them are dishonest.'

'Neither's Sorrel.' Charlie heaved himself to his feet and joined her at the desk. 'You see, I *know* these designs are the ones Sorrel brought to you that day, so if you're denyin' any other explanation you're as good as sayin' you're the rogue as snitched 'em.'

'We're just going round in circles.' Lucas too got to his feet.

'Please, just bear with me a bit longer.' Charlie raised a placating hand. 'Would you mind telling me who, on your staff, claims credit for these designs?'

For a moment it seemed he wasn't going to answer, then, 'My head of design,' he said stiffly.

Sorrel let out a long breath. 'Miss Killingley!' It made sense that the woman would do as her boss asked, and thinking about it, someone in the design department would have to be in on the theft.

'And would she 'ave been present when you read that letter from Sorrel's father?' Charlie pressed.

'She was there when I read the letter *purporting* to be from Mr Valentine, yes,' Lucas agreed stiffly.

'So she'd know as Sorrel 'ad been discredited,' Charlie mused. 'A factor that'd make it a lot less of a risk to get the designs copied an' pass 'em off as 'er own. Possible, don't you think?'

'Possible, but highly improbable,' Sorrel interjected. 'He's in it right up to his neck, Charlie. The pair of them have probably done it before. But they'll be sorry they tried it on with me.'

'Threatening me, Sorrel?' Lucas looked down at her from his greater height, one eyebrow lifted sardonically, and the air fairly sizzled between.

'It's Miss Valentine to you,' she snarled, 'And you bet your sweet life I am. First thing in the morning I'm getting in touch with my solicitor. Nobody pirates *my* work with impunity. I'll make your reputation stink!'

'Your solicitor? I doubt the neighbourhood legal aid office opens on Sunday,' he said insultingly, but Sorrel only smiled, thinking of the high-powered Mr Forster and his swish chambers in Lincoln's Inn Fields, whose percentage from the investments he handled for her put quite a bit of jam on his bread. She didn't think she would have any trouble talking to him on a Sunday. And as he knew all the facts concerning her parentage, she wouldn't have any difficulty convincing him of the seriousness of her charge of piracy against Lucas Amory.

'Perhaps you should find yourself a good solicitor at that,' he advised in such a hatefully superior manner that Sorrel longed to hit him. 'Because first thing in the morning *I* shall be putting the whole thing in the hands of the police.'

'Mr Amory, I'm sure that won't be necessary——' Charlie once again tried to play the peace-maker, but Sorrel had the bit between her teeth.

'You do that, Mr Amory.' Moving quickly she swept the disputed designs into the top drawer, locked it, and much to Lucas Amory's surprise, handed him the key. 'Just to make sure the evidence is where it should be when the police came to investigate,' she taunted. 'And my solicitor will see to it the police get equal co-operation from Amoroso.'

For a few moments he looked nonplussed, but quickly recovered. 'Very well, and now I'm going home.' His chin jutted challengingly at Charlie who was hovering between him and the door, still making placating noises. 'Are you going to stop me?'

'Sorrel . . . ' Charlie made one last attempt.

She waved a dismissive hand. 'Let him go, Charlie. My solicitor will know where to find him.'

She watched as, his back stiff with anger, Lucas Amory strode out of her apartment.

CHAPTER FIVE

'SORREL, I don't think you should've done that,' Charlie said worriedly. 'Threatened 'im with the law, I mean. You know Tammy an' me'll vouch that they *are* your designs, but are they goin' to take our word against Lucas Amory's?'

'Oh, they won't take Mr Amory's word.' Sorrel began to smile. 'Not once they find that letter from my father was absolutely genuine, and . . . ' her smile widened into a grin of pure glee ' . . . that I can *prove* the designs are mine.'

'You can prove it? 'ow, for pity's sake?'

'Charlie, think. I started working on those designs last winter, right? And I made some prototypes, the first of which I gave to my sister for Christmas. *Christmas,* Charlie, so it has last year's date letter on the hallmark, proving without a shadow of a doubt it was made months before Lucas Amory claims I stole his designs.'

Charlie started to chuckle, and moments later they were laughing so hard they had to cling together for support.

'But why the 'ell didn't you floor 'im with that while 'e was 'ere?' Charlie demanded when he had breath enough to speak. 'I'd've loved to see 'is face when 'e 'ad to back-track on those accusations of 'is.'

Sorrel sobered quickly. 'So would I, Charlie, and I still hope to. But it's only my originals that are safely locked in that drawer. Lucas Amory still has the copies he took and he's planning to put them into production. I need the law on my side to put a stop to his gallop. Apart from that . . . ' her mouth twitched upward ' . . . I thought the higher I let that self-righteous male chauvinist climb, the further he'd have to fall.'

'Yes, I noticed the air fairly crackled between you,' Charlie said thoughtfully. 'It'll be interestin' to see what develops once the pair of you 'ave ironed this tangle out.'

Sorrel stared. 'What are you on about, Charlie? Once this is sorted out, if he's not in gaol then I hope I never set eyes on him again.'

'Come on, darlin'.' He put a great arm around her shoulders. 'This is Charlie, remember? I saw the way 'e was eyein' you when you weren't gettin' up 'is nose. And don't try to tell me you didn't find 'im a tasty morsel, either.'

'A tasty morsel! That crook? That arrogant, nasty-minded, womanising, devious . . . I can't find anything bad enough to describe him. I'd have to be starving before I found *him* tasty!'

Charlie started to laugh. ' "The lady doth protest too much, methinks . . . " and all that.'

He was still laughing when Tammy burst in breathlessly. 'I *did* see him leaving, didn't I? Lucas Amory? What's happened? Something has or he wouldn't have stayed all this time. Does he want your——'

Sorrel groaned. 'You tell her, Charlie. I couldn't bear to go over it all again. All I want is my bed.'

She urged them through the door, Tammy still asking questions. Minutes later she was tucked under her duvet, exhaustion closing her eyelids. But for all that she had every reason to distrust and dislike Lucas Amory, in the last few moments before sleep overwhelmed her, she found herself remembering the feel of his mouth against her skin as he had kissed her hand.

Sorrel woke the next morning with the crusading determination to call her solicitor at the earliest possible moment. The sooner she set retribution in motion for Mr Lucas bloody Amory the better, she told herself savagely. But somewhere deep down in her consciousness she was aware that she *needed* to keep fuelling her indignation. If she kept reminding herself how dangerous and unscrupulous he was, it was easier to deny the attraction Charlie had charged her with last night.

Throwing back the duvet, she shrugged on her robe and, barefoot, skipped lightly down the spiral staircase to the kitchen where she put on a large pot of coffee. The weak March sunlight filtering through the sea-green curtains made her sitting-room appear as mysterious as an underwater cavern, and the analogy suddenly made her think of the shapes and textures of sea creatures and coral as an idea for a new range of jewellery. She grinned to herself as she crossed to the three large windows, flinging back the curtains to let in the sun. As upsetting as the bitter battle with Lucas Amory had been last night, it seemed to have unlocked some secret spring inside herself and the ideas were beginning to flow.

Standing as she did every morning at her window, she gazed out on to the slow-moving river. This morning it was in a playful mood, the sunlight catching each facet the brisk easterly wind broke on the surface, giving the impression of glittering fish scales. And once again her creative imagination stirred, mentally converting what her eyes were seeing into the possibilities for a piece of jewellery. The next moment she was at her drawing-board, her pencil moving swiftly as she began to capture her ideas on paper. The coffee percolator had been plopping and gasping for some time before it impinged on her senses.

After three cups of strong coffee and a bowl of muesli and fruit, she soaked in a scented bath. Not even for her would Mr Forster welcome being disturbed so early on a Sunday morning, but with the confidence that he *would* by willing to see her, even on his day of rest, she dressed carefully, choosing a fine wool dress in her favourite bronze-green, the fabric so soft it clung flatteringly to her figure before flaring into fullness round her knees. Her thick mane of russet hair she swept high and smooth, restraining the curl to a few tendrils around her face, a style that was both businesslike and elegant, as well as having the advantage of displaying her dramatic ear-rings —discs of gold fringed with fine chain, each chain tipped with a tiny diamond. Her make-up she kept light as she preferred, but dramatised her eyes with bronze shadow and lengthened her lashes with mascara.

High-heeled bronze shoes completed the ensemble, and Sorrel surveyed the unfamiliar image with an even more pronounced gleam of self-mockery. Very different from her usual uniform of jeans and sweat shirt, but she knew her expensive lawyer would feel more comfortable with *this* Sorrel Valentine. Her glance slid sideways to the portrait Charlie had painted of her. It was a head and shoulders portrait, but he had painted her face—the face she turned to the world with its expression of tolerant amusement—as a hand-held mask, lifted a little away to reveal the same features but bearing the expression of a lost, lonely, frightened child. She grimaced wryly, her finery suddenly seeming the sham it was, only glad the dapper Mr Forster would never see through her with the percipience that was Charlie's.

At ten-thirty she judged she could contact Mr Forster without dragging him from his slumbers, only to have his answering machine tell her he was away on a long weekend but hoped to be back Monday night. There was nothing she could do but leave the message asking for an appointment first thing on Tuesday morning, and try to contain her frustration.

Work seemed the best antidote, and she had once

more immersed herself at her drawing-board when the entry-phone buzzed imperiously. Absent-mindedly she went to ask the identity of her visitor.

'Lucas Amory,' a voice returned tinnily, and Sorrel's heart gave a sudden jerk. This was it, then. He had returned with police reinforcements and she couldn't reach her solicitor before tomorrow night.

Pressing the button to release the lock downstairs, she instructed him to see the door was fastened again before he came up, then after a moment's hesitation, dialled Charlie's number.

He answered sleepily, snapping abruptly awake when Sorrel said, 'Lucas Amory's back, Charlie. I've just let him in.'

His expletive singed her ears. ' 'as 'e brought the law?'

'He didn't say, but I should think it's likely.'

'Whatever, Tammy an' me'll be over.' He hung up noisily.

But when Sorrel opened her front door it was to see Lucas Amory standing there alone. Today there was no suggestion of the dark-suited businessman she had first met, nor of the formality of last night. He was wearing light-coloured slacks and a fawn blouson jacket of a soft suede her fingers itched to touch. And even casually dressed he lost none of his forceful attraction.

Again her heart picked up an uneven beat, and to cover this uncomfortable reaction she made a play of looking behind him, asking, sardonically, 'Where are they? Your cohorts of police?'

He stepped forward, forcing her to retreat. 'As little in evidence as your solicitor,' he said, surveying her empty apartment.

'Unfortunately, my solicitor is a devotee of the country weekend,' she retorted wryly, watching his eyebrows rise.

You *have* tried to contact him then?' His tone

implied his belief that a solicitor was a figment of her imagination.

'Oh, indeed I have. And I've left a message for him to see me as soon as he gets back.' She watched his eyebrows climb higher still. 'So if you haven't come to have me thrown into gaol forthwith, can I hope you've had second thoughts and have come to confess your piracy?'

'Lady, you have style.' He smiled, showing white, even teeth, his dark eyes gleaming in appreciation, a smile that again made Sorrel's heart behave most erratically. 'But no, having no sins to confess—at least not the one you're referring to. Where's the boyfriend this morning?' Disconcertingly he switched the topic.

'As Charlie told you last night, he's Tammy's man. And they'll both be here in a minute,' she added.

'OK, we'll wait.' He walked over to the high windows and looked out, then turned back to survey the room. 'It's amazing what you've done with this place. I like it.'

'Why, thank you, Mr Amory.' Her mocking brown eyes told him she didn't give a damn for his opinion and he smiled again as if that amused him.

'Our acquaintance might be a little . . . unconventional, but I think you could call me Luc.'

Sorrel widened her eyes in counterfeit alarm. 'Oh, I wouldn't dare, not after being put so firmly in my place last night.'

'I'm sorry you feel so . . . overawed by me,' he insinuated wickedly, enjoying her indignant flush. 'I'll just have to work on it, won't I?'

'Before or after your attempt to have me wrongly convicted?' she retorted smartly, and he threw back his head and laughed.

She found herself staring at the strong column of his throat, fascinated by his uninhibited laughter. This was a different man to the one who had been so scathing and insulting last night. Oh, he was still far too sure of himself, still too confident that he could arrange the world to suit himself, but she was in danger of actually finding him likeable.

The surge of adrenalin which was the body's in-built method of dealing with danger had her moving restlessly to her drawing-board. 'I wish you'd tell me why you're here,' she complained. 'I have work to do.'

'Isn't Sunday a day of rest and recreation?' he queried, coming to look over her shoulder. 'These weren't here last night.'

'Us forgers and copyists don't have time to rest,' she retorted sarcastically. 'And no, they weren't here last night because I only got the idea this morning.'

'This morning? It looks to me as if you didn't go to bed.' He flicked back over the pages she had covered, some of the sketches just a few rapidly drawn lines to capture an idea, some drawn in more detail with accompanying notes suggesting finishes or gemstones.

'Only a couple of hours' work,' she dismissed.

'I told you last night,' a voice said behind them, 'once the ideas start flowin', they ooze out of 'er pores.' Charlie, with Tammy tucked comfortably beneath one arm, had come in quietly.

'You dirty, rotten skunk!' Tammy advanced towards her quarry like some vengeful Valkyrie. 'I'd never have landed Sorrel with you if I'd known. You're mad, making such accusations! Let me tell you, Sorrel's the straightest kid I know.' She stopped within inches of Luc, her bosom heaving, her expression promising retribution.

'No fuzz?' Charlie questioned, an element of relief in his voice.

'No police—yet,' Luc concurred.

'Then you'll have come this morning to apologise to Sorrel,' Tammy stated, meeting him eye to eye.

'Not so as you'd notice,' Sorrel muttered.

'No, I haven't gone that far.' A fugitive amusement lurked in his eyes.

'So why have you come?' Tammy was by no means ready to back off yet.

'I wanted to discover Sorrel's reaction to a telephone conversation I've had this morning with the head of my design department.' The amusement was gone and his voice was clipped.

'Ah . . . the incorruptible Miss Killingley,' Charlie murmured.

'As you say, the incorruptible Miss Killingley who was, quite naturally, horrified at the suggestion that she would ever be so unethical as to steal another designer's work.'

'I'm sure she doesn't find it nearly so hard to believe the *boss* of Amoroso could be so unethical,' Sorrel said sourly.

Disappointingly he refused to rise to her bait. 'And she was even more horrified when she had to admit her carelessness could have made it possible for you to steal copies of her designs,' he finished softly.

'Indeed?' Knowing she had proof of her innocence enabled Sorrel to stay calm. 'I'd be interested to hear what story she came up with.'

'First of all, she maintains the designs you brought in were quite unremarkable, derivative . . . lacking any originality.'

Tammy exploded with disgust right under his nose. 'Sorrel's never produced an unoriginal piece of work in her life!'

But Luc was watching Sorrel intently and took no notice of the interruption. 'She also maintains that, although she hadn't connected the disappearance of a set of photocopies of those now disputed designs with your visit to her office, she admits they had been left openly on her desk, and that you were alone in her office while you were waiting for the return of the designs I had just turned down.'

'Then unless you're making it up, or you fed her the words to say, she's lying through her teeth.' Sorrel held her head proudly, her eyes fearless as they clashed with his.

Neither Charlie nor Tammy spoke, as if understanding their opinions were superfluous in this battle of wills. And if Sorrel had the fugitive hope that the third of her suppositions was the correct one—that Miss Killingley was lying and that she was tricking Luc as surely as she was tricking Sorrel—she thrust it away. The battle was silent, neither giving an inch, the tension mounting until the very air between them seemed to quiver.

It was Luc who broke it, not giving in but rather changing course. 'I think it's time for a confrontation, don't you?' he said softly.

Sorrel blinked as what he was suggesting sank in, then agreed with considerable relish, 'It can't be too soon for me. I've quite a few things to say to your "incorruptible" Miss Killingley.'

'Then shall we go?' he invited blandly, a tone that, had she known him better, would have made her suspect he was up to something.

But, unsuspecting, Sorrel was already half-way to the door, picking up her handbag from the sofa, saying over her shoulder, 'There's a pot roast ready to pop into the microwave, Tam, if you'd like to stay and eat. I'll have mine cold with pickles when I get back.'

'I'd have thought a beautiful girl like you would have a husband and family to cook for by now,' Luc remarked as he opened the passenger door of the sleek Mercedes. And when she still hadn't responded as he pulled out into the desultory Sunday morning traffic, 'Well? Why don't you have a husband and family to look after?'

'I doubt if it's for the same reason you don't have

a wife and family to support,' she answered obliquely, and he laughed.

'All right, let's begin there. Why do you think I don't have a wife?'

'Because there are too many women eager to give you the benefits without any of the drawbacks,' she retorted promptly.

'And just what would you say *were* those benefits and drawbacks?'

'In your case? The benefit of access to many women's beds without the drawback of having to commit yourself to only one.' It wasn't easy to make the statement without allowing a blush to crawl up her cheeks.

He shook his head as if hurt by her low opinion. 'And what would you say if I told you I'd welcome a commitment if only I could find that special woman I could love?' he asked softly.

Sorrel's stomach seemed to roll right over and, just for a few moments, her wayward imagination was putting herself in the place of that special woman. This time she was unable to control the blush that reddened her cheeks. 'I'd say either you haven't been looking very hard or you're particularly hard to please if you haven't found her in forty years.'

He frowned. 'You're determined to make me out a dirty old man, aren't you? As a matter of fact I'm four years short of forty. How about you? Rather more than that, I guess.'

'More than forty? I'm twenty-six!' Outraged, she fell neatly into his trap.

He grinned. 'I meant more than four years short of forty, of course. So, if you don't have the same reason for remaining unmarried as you believe I have, I'd be interested to know it.'

Sorrel kept her lips folded.

'You don't sleep around?'

This was too much. 'Like you, you mean? No, I

don't, so you needn't come up with any more pointed allusions to Charlie.'

'Having seen the redoubtable Tammy on the war-path, I'm willing to admit I was way off-beam there,' he conceded magnanimously. 'But no other special man in your life?'

'Perhaps I'm like you and haven't found the one I could love yet,' she returned waspishly, this conversation making her feel uncomfortable.

While they had been talking the car had been covering the ground effortlessly. Looking around her she thought they could be heading towards Highgate or Hampstead. 'Where are we going?' she asked belatedly.

'You'll see when we get there. So, if we're both looking for the right partner, there could be hope for us yet,' he pursued.

'Us? Oh come on, I'm a forger, a liar, a cheat and a thief, remember,' she hooted, but her insides had turned to the consistency of warm butter.

'You said it!' The car slowed to turn in between impressive gateposts.

'Wow!' Sorrel found herself looking at the white façade of a house standing in at least an acre of closely shaved lawns where daffodils tossed their heads in immaculate beds and a large forsythia sprawled over one side of a treble garage. 'There must be a lot of money to be made pirating other designers' work if Miss Killingley can afford to live in *this* style!'

Luc was looking at her very strangely but as she unclipped her seat-belt she was too busy noticing how many other cars there were parked in the drive. 'Oh lord, she's got company,' she muttered. 'Do you think we ought——'

'It's only a drinks party.' He gripped her arm and urged her towards the front door which was standing a little ajar. 'Surely you're not going to back out now.'

Shrugging off her misgivings, she allowed him to

lead her into a large hall that seemed to be crammed
with people. A sudden uneasiness raised the hairs on
the back of her neck, though there was nothing in the
restrained opulence of the décor and furnishings to
account for it, an uneasiness that increased when she
realised Luc had closed the door behind them as if
cutting off her retreat. A number of people greeted
him but he didn't pause to introduce her, and Sorrel
looked around for Miss Killingley, wanting to get this
confrontation over so she could leave. But the only
familiar face she saw was that of Bianca Fratelli, and
almost at the same moment the model spotted Sorrel's
companion.

'Luc!' The crowd seemed to part for her as she
threw herself into his arms, hugging him delightedly.
'I thought you told me you weren't going to make it!'

The English public school accent coming from a
girl who looked so completely Italian was nearly as
much of a shock to Sorrel as the wave of pure jealousy
at the tender amusement on Luc's face as he bent to
kiss the girl's smooth cheek.

She turned, smiling, to Sorrel. 'I don't know how
you got him here, but obviously your persuasion was
more effective than mine.'

'Oh, but——' Sorrel slanted an embarrassed glance
at Luc, expecting him to explain her presence to his
girl-friend. When he didn't, she stammered, 'A-actually
this isn't a social occasion, more sort of business——'

'Of course!' The dark girl's eyes widened in recognition. 'I've been puzzling over where I've seen you
before. It was in Luc's office several weeks ago, wasn't
it?' A mischievous smile made her piquant face look
positively impish. 'Oh, I bet he didn't enjoy having to
admit he was wrong!' And then, at Sorrel's blank face,
'You have sorted that business of the letter out,
haven't you? You must have done or you'd hardly be
here.'

'Bianca, darling, you're talking too much as usual,'

Luc drawled, pretending not to notice Sorrel's puzzled glance. 'As Sorrel says, we have a little matter of business to dispose of, then I'll be back.' He was turning Sorrel away from the model when she caught sight of another familiar face across the room, deeply tanned now after his month in Barbados, the grey eyes staring at her in horrified recognition.

Every muscle in her body stiffened into rigidity as it all fell into place. Time for a confrontation, Luc had said, and she had assumed he'd meant Miss Killingley. 'This is my father's house,' she accused him in a stricken voice.

'It's Felix Valentine's home,' he mocked hatefully. 'As you would have known had you really been his daughter.'

Sorrel closed her eyes, as if by cutting out the scene it might disappear like a bad dream. 'You don't understand . . . ' she muttered, then more forcefully, 'I must go!'

But Luc's hand clamped painfully round her arm. 'Oh, no you don't, you little cheat. You'll stay and face the music.'

She flung back her head to stare at him contemptuously, unaware of Bianca or any of the other Sunday morning party-goers who might be listening. 'My father may eventually forgive you for this, Lucas Amory, but I never shall!'

A muscle twitched in his jaw, but like a juggernaut he rolled imperviously on, not deviating from his purpose or relaxing his grip on her arm as they waited for the man hurrying towards them.

'Sorrel, for God's sake, what are you doing here?' Her father's hoarse undertone scraped along her nerves. 'You promised you'd see Luc was discreet.'

'I'm sorry, Father, but Mr Amory has been playing games.' She held herself proudly, refusing to be cowed or even embarrassed. 'I had no idea it was your house he was bringing me to.'

'I don't understand . . . ' Harassed, with not a shred of his usual cool dispassion remaining, Felix Valentine looked at his frozen-faced friend.

'It's quite simple,' Sorrel said. 'Mr Amory didn't believe you wrote that letter for me. He believes I forged it.'

'Oh, hell!' Perspiration stood out in beads on her father's forehead.

'Felix . . . ' Luc's voice sounded strangled. 'You mean she really——'

'Don't look so worried, Father,' Sorrel cut across him rudely. 'I would have left as soon as I realised if Mr Amory had allowed it. And if you'll ask him to unhand me, I'll go at once.'

She felt Luc's hand jerk away as if he'd been scalded, while red slid beneath her father's tan. 'Damnation! It doesn't seem right to turn you out of my home, my dear, only Marcia . . . '

But retreat was too late. A slender woman of supreme elegance, her grey hair cut into a carefully casual style, was already bearing down on them, eyes only for Luc Amory, smile and hands extended in welcome.

'Luc, my dear man! We haven't had a glimpse of you since before we went away.' She put her cheek up for his kiss, then turning to Sorrel with a politely welcoming expression, her face froze. *'You!'* Rounding furiously on her husband she hissed, 'Did you ask her here? Without telling me? How *could* you! You promised . . . '

Suddenly Sorrel had had enough of them all, the arrogance of Luc Amory who didn't care who got hurt as long as he did things his way, the rather pathetic weakness of her father, Marcia's obsession with old grudges. 'There's no need to browbeat my father in public, Marcia,' she drawled, uncaring who heard. 'The responsibility lies entirely with your dear friend Mr Amory. And now he's had his fun, I'll leave.' Nodding frostily at the outraged Marcia and her distinctly uncomfortable father, and ignoring Luc completely, she turned away, only to feel once more his hand on her arm.

'I'll take you home, Sorrel,' he said stiffly.

'You will *not!*' The look she gave him should have stunned anybody at twenty paces.

He released her arm but persisted stubbornly. 'I brought you here.'

'So you did.' Her lip curled contemptuously. 'And now you should stay and explain why you were so keen to cause my father and stepmother such embarrassment.'

With unconscious dignity she turned and walked out of her father's house. And Luc let her go.

CHAPTER SIX

ONCE again the outsider, Sorrel thought bitterly as she stalked down the drive. Well, she could get along without her father *or* Luc Amory. She'd done it before and she'd do it again. They were brave words but they didn't stop her hurting.

Indignation and pride kept her warm as she walked along the residential road lined with houses ranging from the quietly luxurious to the ostentatiously opulent, but she had left home without a coat and, by the time she reached the end of the road, she was shivering in the cool March wind.

She had passed the Spaniards, a famous pub she'd heard of but never visited, when a car pulling up beside her had her whirling defensively, not the Mercedes she'd feared but a snazzy red sports car, though the girl sliding out was only too familiar.

'Sorrel, do let me run you home,' Bianca begged.

Sorrel was staggered to see her, then unreasonably angry. 'I suppose *he* sent you. Do you always jump to his bidding, Miss Fratelli?'

The dark girl grimaced. 'Bianca, *please*. And you don't have to tell *me* how bloody-minded Luc can be, though he's not nearly so bad when you get to know him.'

If Sorrel found it strange that Luc Amory's girl-friend should have come after her to offer her help, or that she should take the trouble to plead in Luc's defence, she was still too upset to think about it. 'But then he hasn't accused you of being a liar and a thief,' she dismissed, 'or implied that if you have a father, you must be a bastard.'

Oddly, the pretty model seemed to flinch at her hard words, and Sorrel felt a stab of compunction. 'I'm sorry. I've no right to vent my spleen on you. Thanks for you offer, but no thanks. I'll pick up a cab in the village.'

'Oh, but Luc said——' Bianca began to protest, and the name was enough to have Sorrel bristling again.

'Please,' she broke in firmly. 'If you want to do something for me, then go back to the party and tell Mr Amory to stop bothering me.'

'But you're shivering, and no wonder, without a coat.' Bianca herself was dressed in a warm wool suit that looked like a Chanel. 'Is it worth getting a chill just to score off Luc? Forget him, and let me take you home for *my* peace of mind, huh?'

And so genuinely concerned did the girl seem that Sorrel found herself folding her long legs into the sports car.

With the heater going full blast, she soon stopped shivering, and when Bianca chatted lightly about a wide range of innocuous subjects, mostly her experiences as a fashion model, she found herself liking the girl, liking her sense of humour, her ability to laugh at herself, her complete lack of affectation. No wonder Luc was often reported and photographed in her company. The wonder was that he was still seen in the company of other women, too. Bianca was very young, of course, and maybe he was afraid of being accused of cradle-snatching, except she couldn't imagine Luc allowing gossip or anything else to stand in his way.

They were passing the Tower of London before Bianca introduced the topic that had thrown them together that day. With a muffled giggle she gurgled, 'I keep seeing Luc's face when he found out Felix

Valentine really *is* your father! No, it's all right,' she hastened to add when Sorrel shifted uncomfortably in her seat, 'I'm not going to ask questions even if I *am* dying of curiosity. It's just that Luc does hate being wrong.'

'I can imagine,' Sorrel said drily, reminded that although she had proved her relationship to Felix Valentine, she still had to prove her claim to her designs. Which meant almost certainly she would have to meet Luc again, a prospect she viewed with mixed feelings.

Monday morning found Sorrel in her work-room by eight-thirty, the issue still unresolved. She had thanked Bianca for bringing her home and had got into her apartment to find Tammy and Charlie still waiting. After explaining the events of the morning and listening to their indignant sympathy, she had tried to settle down with her sketch-book, but had found herself listening for the buzz of her entry-phone which would herald Luc Amory's arrival. So sure had she been that he would try to see her, if only to apologise for all the insulting names he'd called her, she could hardly believe it when bedtime came and she'd still heard no word.

If he thought that was the end of the matter and he had got away with stealing her designs, he had another think coming, she told herself angrily. Mr Forster might still be away until tonight, but there was nothing to stop her calling his chambers and getting one of his minions to slap an injunction on Amoroso. And in the meantime, physical work fitted her mood.

Pulling her stool into the concave curve in her work-bench and making sure the chamois leather apron beneath the curve was securely in place to catch any fragments of precious metal that fell, she took out her current piece of work from the drawer. It was a silver christening bracelet, commissioned and due for collection in a couple of days; six dainty spring flowers, each one different. The individual pieces had been returned from the assay office on Friday, and beside the assay stamp, each also bore Sorrel's mark, the entwined SV. On Friday she had done the hand finishing, and now all that remained to be done was to link the pieces together and give them their final polishing.

Putting everything else out of her mind she set to work with jeweller's glass, needle-flame gas torch and silver solder to join the tiny links. It was intricate work but Sorrel's fingers moved deftly, her concentration absolute, so when a hand descended on her shoulder she jumped visibly.

'I'm sorry,' Luc Amory said. 'I didn't mean to startle you.'

'Well, you did. You nearly gave me heart failure.' Her heart was still slamming against her ribs, but there was an element of excitement mixed in with the shock. Not wanting to admit this to herself she said disagreeably, 'What are you doing here, anyway? Creeping in to see if I've got any more designs worth stealing?'

'You knew I'd be back,' he said with his unassailable confidence.

'Well, I did rather expect at least a phone call yesterday,' she said with heavy irony. 'If only with an overdue apology.'

'Were you disappointed, Sorrel?' His dark eyes mocked her but the intimacy in his tone sent her stomach into another roll. Worse, she was very well aware that her most predominant emotion yesterday *had* been disappointment.

'As a matter of fact——' Luc picked up the bracelet she had been working on, examining it as he spoke. '—I wanted to come yesterday but I was afraid you wouldn't let me through the door. I thought if I left it till this morning your righteous indignation might have spent itself.'

Righteous indignation! The man was so arrogant he made even an apology sound like an insult. 'And don't you think I had the right to be indignant?' she demanded. 'I'm sure it took a much more convincing apology than the one you've just given me to smooth down Marcia's feathers.'

To her surprise he said quietly, 'Yes, you had every reason to be upset, not only with my insensitive method of getting at the truth but also with the treatment you received from your father and step-mother. And I haven't even begun my apology yet.' He laid down the bracelet and glanced at his watch. 'Trouble is, time's getting on. I've left instructions for Miss Killingley to present herself in my office at nine-thirty, so if we're not to be hopelessly late, we should be going.'

'*We* should be going?' Sorrel echoed faintly. 'I—I had intended to leave the recovery of my designs to my lawyer. I know Mr Forster isn't there but someone in his office can begin the process of taking out an injunction.'

'Forster?' Luc's expressive eyebrows signified his shock. 'Of Forster and Stalbridge?'

'You know him?' The idea was unwelcome. Wouldn't it just be her luck if he was Luc's solicitor, too!

'I know *of* him.' He was frowning. 'At least, I know he's one of the top men, and he doesn't come cheap.'

'No,' Sorrel agreed. 'He's been looking after my affairs since I was a child.'

'Well, you can still get your injunction later, if necessary,' he suggested disconcertingly. 'But you could save yourself a lot of money if we can resolve our dispute without resorting to the law. It shouldn't be too difficult. Both you and Eve Killingley claim those designs. One of you has to be lying. If it's Eve, don't you want to see her get her just desserts?'

It was enough to galvanise her into action. Dropping the bracelet into a drawer and locking it, she said, 'Have I got time to change?'

Smothering his smile of satisfaction Luc said, 'No, you don't, and anyway . . . ' His gaze travelled over her long, jean-clad legs to the soft swell of her breasts beneath the bias stripes of the hand-knitted mohair sweater. 'You look delicious enough already.'

'Now for the apology,' Luc said when they were in the car and immediately embroiled in the slow-moving traffic. 'Looking at it from my point of view, you must admit your sudden appearance with that letter was very suspicious, when in all the years I've known Felix, I never had a hint of a previous marriage, let alone a daughter. But having said that, I *could* have checked your credentials, even while Felix was in Barbados, before laying into you and calling you names. I'm sorry for that, and I'm even more sorry for the distress I caused you yesterday. It must have been most unpleasant and hurtful, having your dirty linen washed in public, and then to be thrown out of your father's house.'

It was a handsome apology, surprisingly perceptive, and it weakened Sorrel's defences. 'I *walked* out, if you remember; I wasn't thrown.' Her sherry-brown eyes were wry. 'And I think Marcia was more distressed by the dirty linen washed than I was.'

He was shaking his head. 'I just had no idea of the situation. And when you didn't even recognise the house . . . '

'Well, of course I didn't, because I'd never been there.' At his look of incredulity she explained, 'I'm not quite sure where we lived while my parents were married, but it wasn't far from Regent's Park Zoo. I was only six when they split up, you see.'

'And naturally you stayed with your mother,' he added thoughtfully.

'No, I went to live in Kent with my godmother,

and didn't see either of my parents for the next three years.' she corrected him.

They were waiting at traffic lights and he shot her a horrified glance. 'Not at *all?*'

She shook her head. 'I can't say I remember missing them. I'd never seen a great deal of them anyway, and then I had Ellie.' Her mouth curved in a reminiscent smile, remembering the pretty house near Canterbury with its sprawling wild garden and the fun it had been with Ellie, the laughter and affection, the *time* Ellie—her father's cousin and a maiden lady of independent means—had always had for her. 'They were certainly the happiest days of my life. But then Ellie became ill.' Her smiled faded. 'She went into hospital and I was sent to boarding school. I never saw her again, wasn't even told she'd died until after the funeral.'

She was silent for a few moments, remembering her childish grief. 'After that, my school holidays were divided between Thorley and London, but by then Mother was a stranger, living in a big house I always found scary, with a husband I was shy with and a baby—Julia—of whom I was horribly jealous.'

'And your father must have remarried and started his second family by then,' Luc commented.

Yes, but I didn't realise it for a long time.' He looked puzzled and she explained, 'The part of my holidays I spent in London I always stayed with Fred Mullins and his family. Fred was—still is—my father's security man. I liked that, far better than staying at Thorley. He had two children, older than me, but they never minded me tagging along. In fact, on the days my father came to take me out, I would much rather have stayed playing with them. Ungrateful of me, I know. I quite liked the visits to the zoo, but it wasn't for several years that I could appreciate the art galleries and museums.' Her wryly cynical smile gleamed like shy sunshine. 'Father wasn't very inspired at thinking up entertainment for a little girl.'

Luc eased the car forward a few yards at a time along Cannon Street, appalled at what he was hearing. If he had bothered to search for a motive for the actions of the girl he'd first taken for an audacious confidence trickster, he supposed he would have put it down to a materially deprived childhood. In fact her childhood and adolescence had been well cushioned materially, the deprivation being something far more important—the love and security that should be every child's by right. 'Didn't your father ever take his sons along on those outings?' he asked. 'Or were they still too young?'

'I told you, I didn't know for a long time he'd even married again,' she said quietly. 'I've still never met his sons.'

'You've never met Justin and Dominic!' he exclaimed incredulously. 'Why not, for heaven's sake? They *are* your brothers.'

Sorrel shrugged. 'That's not a fact Marcia likes to be reminded of, and Father doesn't like to upset her. It's understandable, I suppose. His first marriage was a disaster, while this one, as far as I know, is happy. I can't blame him for not wanting to rock the boat.'

They were sweeping round St Paul's Cathedral now and into Newgate Street, speeding up over the Viaduct but getting snarled up again as they approached Holborn Circus and the turning into Hatton Garden. 'Well, I can!' Luc said forcefully, shocked at this new perspective of his long-time friends. 'You're his *daughter,* for God's sake! I don't understand him at all, or Marcia's attitude towards you for that matter.'

Sorrel found his championing of her both surprising and heart-warming. 'There are reasons, Luc.' After a moment's hesitation she went on to sketch in the story her father had told her some weeks before. 'I suppose Marcia always saw it as a betrayal, something she doesn't like to be reminded of, hence her aversion to me.'

Luc considered her reasoning, then rejected it. 'I don't buy that. Marcia's an adult, a mature, sophisticated woman. I see neither reason nor logic in bearing a grudge for so many years, certainly not against you, who've done nothing to hurt her.'

What he was saying was true, but emotions were not susceptible to either reason or logic. And Sorrel was beginning to feel a stirring of alarm. It wouldn't help her already shaky relationship with her father if he felt she had turned Luc against him. 'Please, Luc,' she said hurriedly, as the car drew to a halt outside the Amoroso building. 'Don't make a big thing of it. After all, they're your friends, while I'm just . . . a chance acquaintance.'

He made no reply but his mouth was set in a grim line as he helped her out before tossing his keys to the doorman. As they travelled up in the lift Sorrel regretted having told him so much. Indeed, she couldn't think how she had come to talk to him about it at all. She never had before, not even to Tammy and Charlie. Sneaking a sideways glance at his still grim expression that gave no clue to what he was thinking, it occurred to her he might see her confidences as a bid for his sympathy in the coming confrontation. The suspicion appalled her and stiffened her pride. She would show him she didn't need his sympathy. *She* was not the one on trial. By the time the lift doors opened she was walking tall, the light of battle in her eyes.

So it was an anticlimax to find, when Luc ushered her into his outer office, only the blonde secretary waiting.

'Where's Miss Killingley?' Luc barked, ignoring the fact that he was nearly half an hour late.

'Oh, she *was* here, Mr Amory.' The flustered secretary rose to her feet. 'But when you were——'

'Get her,' he rapped, opening the door into his

private office and motioning Sorrel inside.

The décor was as modern as the outer office, but surprisingly spartan for a man she had judged to be fond of his creature comforts, a huge desk dominating the room, a capacious chair suitable for a man of his size behind it and only two others, neither of which looking as if they encouraged lounging. No pictures or even photographs of Amoroso products on the walls, just charts and a huge wall planner which seemed to show where not only Luc himself but all other key members of his staff should be at any one time. An office for working in, with no distractions.

The only apparent concession to comfort was a coffee-maker standing on a table against one wall, its pot full and keeping warm on a hotplate. Luc immediately made for it, pouring two cups and handing her one as he indicated one of the chairs drawn up in front of the desk. Sorrel was pleased to see how steady her hand was as she took it. Luc must have noticed too, for he said, 'You're not nervous.'

'I have no reason to be,' she retorted with a composure that didn't waver one iota as he subjected her to his darkly searching scrutiny.

'Why do I get the feeling you know something I don't? he asked softly, but before she could think up a reply there was a tap at the door and Miss Killingley walked in.

'I'm sorry I didn't wait, Luc,' she gushed. 'But not knowing how long you were going to be delayed . . . ' Her voice died away and her eager-to-please expression faded as she saw and recognised Sorrel.

'You very sensibly got on with some work,' Luc finished for her. 'It's I who should be apologising for being so late. You've met Miss Valentine, haven't you? Will you have some coffee before we sort out this unfortunate muddle?' He filled another cup. 'Do sit down, Eve.'

The woman who had blanched on seeing Sorrel,

recovered quickly at her boss's friendly welcome.
Taking the cup of coffee, she perched on the edge of
the other chair. 'Muddle, Luc?' She gave a strained
laugh. 'You're being kind if you're referring to my
criminal negligence in leaving those photocopies of
the new range lying around.'

Sorrel watched closely, a sick feeling in the pit of
her stomach, while Luc gave his designer a wryly
understanding smile and walked round to sit behind
the desk. It wasn't that she was any less confident of
being able to prove her ownership of the designs, it
was that only now, seeing him showing Miss Killingley
such support and partisanship, did she realise that for
some time—probably since yesterday morning—she
had unconsciously acquitted him of having a hand in
stealing them. Now, suddenly she was not so sure,
and the disappointment in him was wrenching.

Elbows resting on the chair arms, his fingers stee-
pled, he said judiciously, 'The purpose of this meeting
is to decide just where the criminality lies. On the one
hand we have a set of designs that you, Eve, claim is
your work, and on the other hand an identical set of
designs which Miss Valentine insists is hers, moreover,
that they are the ones she brought here last month for
my consideration and which I—foolishly as it turns
out—declined to look at. Now Miss Valentine claims
you *did* look at them, Eve, so perhaps you will
describe them to me.'

'I—well yes I did look at them—briefly. But it was
some weeks ago and I don't know that I remember—'
Eve Killingley floundered.

Luc leaned forward. 'Bear with me, Eve. If I'm to
get to the bottom of this little plot I need to know all
the details.'

Stumblingly Eve began to describe necklaces and
bracelet, rings and ear-rings, like nothing Sorrel had
ever put her name to. 'As I told you on the phone
yesterday, Luc, there was nothing original about any

Secrets of Love.

Dare you unlock these pages of sensual Temptation?

Discover your own **FREE** *Gift…*

Dare you experience TEMPTATION?

Naked love...powerful, provocative, sensual...

That is the theme of Mills & Boon's Temptation series – when the chemistry between a man and a woman is so overwhelming that they cannot resist the touch...the kiss...the embrace that sets light to the senses. And when love is ignited, every aspect of their lives changes...

Told with the candour, the honesty and realism – and the tenderness – of some of our most appreciated authors, the Temptation Experience could be for *you*.

And now you can sample FOUR FREE TEMPTATION NOVELS in your own home. Yours to keep even if you never buy a single novel!

We will also reserve a subscription for you, so that you can continue to receive six brand-new Temptation titles every other month. PLUS free membership of Mills & Boon Reader Service – the privilege that brings you all the exciting benefits detailed overleaf.

It's an astonishing no-risk offer – with a Free Gift too!

Don't resist a moment longer –
Fill in your claim card NOW!

Yes Please send me my FOUR FREE TEMPTATION NOVELS as soon as possible, without any charges for post and packing.

Yes I would also like to receive my own Free Gift Digital Quartz Clock.

Yes Please reserve a Reader Service subscription for me so that I can enjoy all these benefits with no obligation to purchase a minimum number of books

- free newsletter packed with author news, free competitions, previews and special book offers
- free postage and packing
- the latest titles reserved for me and delivered direct to my door

Remember, *your Free Gift and your Four Free Temptation novels are yours to keep* **without obligation!**

Reader Service
FREEPOST
PO Box 236
Croydon
SURREY
CR9 9EL.

of it, nothing that would stick in the memory.'

'Odd then, that there was nothing remotely like what you describe in the work I saw at Sorrel's studio,' Luc said reflectively, and Sorrel's eyes narrowed, her heart giving a perceptible lift.

'Well, I've admitted my memory isn't infallible.' Eve's tongue flicked out to moisten her lips, and then she rushed into the attack. 'All I *do* know for sure is that that set of photocopies hasn't been seen since Miss Valentine was last in my office. Or is she denying she was ever alone in there?' She flung that last challenge straight at Sorrel.

'Miss Valentine?' Luc looked at her questioningly. 'Do you have anything to say in your defence?'

'I don't deny I was alone in Miss Killingley's office for about five minutes while I waited for the return of my designs,' Sorrel said quietly. 'But I saw no photocopies. In fact, if any copying was done, it was by Miss Killingley over the three days my work was in her possession.'

'You can't possibly believe that!' Eve appealed to Luc. 'The word of someone who tried to bring herself to your notice with a forged letter?'

'And if it wasn't forged?' Luc asked gently.

'Well, of course it was. I was there when you said so, and you've known Mr Valentine long enough to know he has no daughter.'

'Long enough, but not well enough it seems. I was wrong, Eve.' His voice was still soft but there was an underlying hint of steel. 'Sorrel *is* Felix Valentine's daughter by an early marriage I didn't know about.'

Eve Killingley opened and closed her mouth several times without finding her voice and perspiration beaded her upper lip.

'I suggest, Eve, that you recognised the quality of Miss Valentine's work—a quality that has been lacking in your own work, as I've had cause to comment——' Luc went on inexorably. 'And that when I made that regrettable mistake in disbelieving Miss Valentine's credentials, you saw your opportunity to make copies of her designs and to pass them off as your own. I suggest that it was only yesterday when I telephoned you that you thought up those conveniently missing photocopies.'

'No . . . no, it's not true . . . none of it. They *are* my designs,' Eve claimed wildly. 'Even if she *is* Felix Valentine's daughter it doesn't mean she's above stealing.' At the open contempt in his face she pleaded tearfully, 'Luc, I've given ten years of my life to this company. Are you going to take *her* word against mine?'

Luc stood up, looking so forbidding even Sorrel quailed, though she was beginning to understand that his soft approach, rather than proving his complicity, had been to lull Eve Killingley into feeling safe before he went in for the kill. 'Eve.' He leaned over the now cowering woman. 'Sorrel can *prove* they are her original designs.'

'Oh God!' Her face crumpled like tissue paper. 'I *knew* I shouldn't have done it. Only with you threatening to replace me . . . Well, you know how I'm placed, with Mother so ill. How could I tell her I'd lost my job? Oh God! I shall have to now, shan't I?' She began to sob noisily.

Sorrel stared down at her clasped hands rather than witness her collapse, hating to feel she was responsible, however indirectly. She knew it was illogical when Eve Killingley had accused her, had possibly even been prepared to press a prosecution, but Sorrel could only feel sorry for her now.

She heard a click and looked up sharply as she heard Luc say into the intercom, 'Alison, will you come in, please?' Surely he wasn't going to expose the poor woman in front of the secretary! But when the girl appeared he merely instructed her to take Miss Killingley to the ladies' room and mop her up, adding,

'I'll talk to her again later, when she's calmed down.'

There was a heavy silence after the door had closed behind the two women, then Luc said, 'I'm sorry, that was . . . nasty.'

'Was it true what she said? That you were threatening to replace her?' Sorrel asked.

He sighed. 'Ten years ago Eve was full of ideas. I had no hesitation in putting her in charge of the department when her predecessor moved on. But the last couple of years . . . She still runs the department competently but the ideas had dried up. Yes, I did threaten to replace her, but only because I thought it might prove a spur.'

'And is it true about her mother being sick?' she pressed.

Frowning, he began to prowl the room. 'Her mother did suffer a stroke, about two years ago as it happens. But Eve has someone to care for her while she's at work.'

'But all the time she's *not* working, she must be nursing her mother herself,' Sorrel suggested. 'All her leisure time. Enough of a drain to sap her creative energy, I'd think. And she can have little opportunity to do as I do, take time to study the past in museums, keep up with other designers' work and watch the trends.'

He stopped his prowling to stand over her, staring as if she was some species he wasn't familiar with. 'You can feel sympathy for her? After what she tried to do to you?'

Sorrel refused to be intimidated by his looming presence. 'I can see what a temptation a foolproof method of impressing you might have been,' she said quietly.

He subsided to perch on the corner of his desk, still too close for Sorrel's comfort. 'Can you, now! You're very good at understanding the motives of others, even when they're trying to hurt you. Tell me, Sorrel, has anyone ever tried to understand *you?*'

A betraying colour crept into her cheeks. 'I don't know what you mean,' she said evasively, then to give his thoughts another direction, 'Why did you tell Eve I could prove those designs were mine? I'd never made any such claim to you.'

'No, you didn't, did you? I wonder why not?' He surveyed her thoughtfully when she didn't answer. 'OK, first you weren't in the least worried when I threatened you with the police. Then you were prepared to set a very expensive lawyer on to me, not to mention that you were ready and eager to confront Eve. You were so confident, there had to be something. Was I right?'

'Oh, you were right.' A smile curved her mouth and her bright eyes mocked him.

'Going to tell me?' he coaxed, his own eyes showing amusement.

'That pendant, the one you recognised on Julia?' She tilted her head questioningly but he still looked blank. 'I gave it to her last Christmas. It was one of my first experiments when I got the idea for the range. The hallmark bears last year's date letter, so couldn't possibly have been made since I was supposed to have stolen the designs.'

He threw back his head and gave such a bellow of laughter the light fittings rattled. 'My God! I *deserve* to have my pride ground in the dust for missing such an obvious point. And just when did you remember that crucial fact yourself, may I ask?'

'Oh, about half-way through our slanging match on Saturday night.' Sorrel was having difficulty controlling her own twitching lips. 'Just before you threatened me with the police, to be precise.'

'You little bitch!' But the epithet was spoken softly, almost as an endearment, occasioning a sudden surge in Sorrel's pulse rate. 'So why didn't you face me with that fact then? Put an end to the argument?'

Sorrel sobered quickly, remembering how threatened she'd felt. 'And have you get to Julia first and destroy the evidence? You'd just kidnapped me, don't forget, forced your way into my home, claimed my designs as yours and were accusing me of stealing them, so it didn't seem to me you'd have any scruples about protecting yourself. Besides, I was furious. I wanted you to fall even deeper into the pit you'd dug for yourself before I buried you.'

' "O wad some Pow'r the giftie gie us, To see oursels as others see us!" ' he quoted ruefully. 'Though I doubt Robert Burns had quite such a situation in mind. All right, seen from your angle I'll accept caution was the best course. But what about your designs now, Sorrel?' He got up and walked over to the wall planner. 'They're still ready to go into production. More than that, the launch is scheduled for . . . ' he ran his finger down the chart. ' . . . seven weeks from now, at a joint showing with Hywel Rees.'

Sorrel's eyes opened wide at the mention of the young Welsh fashion designer who had hit the headlines only last year. Luc turned back to her. 'Are we going to be able to come to some arrangement?'

Oddly enough, Sorrel hadn't thought beyond proving her title to the designs, but now excitement and elation gripped her. Wasn't this what she'd hoped for when she'd first tried to meet Luc? That he would take her up and make her name as a designer? But there had been too many disappointments in her life, too many situations that had turned sour, to believe in a dream come true. He could be offering nothing more than payment for the designs while Amoroso took all the credit.

'What kind of arrangement?' she asked cautiously.

'That contract I would have offered had we not had our unfortunate . . . misunderstanding.' He smiled, then seating himself again behind his desk, enlarged briskly, 'A down-payment for the use of your designs and a retainer for your advice and instruction up to the launch, plus a royalty on subsequent sales—the percentage to be negotiated. Also the use of your name to promote the launch in all our publicity.'

Sorrel drew an audible breath. It was all she had ever hoped for. She was aware of Luc watching her, expecting her to jump at his offer. And she was going to, of course. But the warmth of his dark gaze made her suspect there was more on offer than he had set out, things of a much more personal nature, and every instinct told her it would be dangerous to become involved with this man.

To give herself time to think she asked, 'What exactly would be involved in this advice and instruction you mention?'

His quizzical smile made her wonder if he suspected the reason for her hesitation. 'Working closely with Hywel Rees co-ordinating your jewellery with his clothes and instructing my production manager on any modifications, making yourself available to the advertising department for pre-publicity, and of course——' his smile widened '—keeping me informed at all times of developments. Everything, in fact, Eve has been doing.'

Sorrel seized on the disgraced designer's name because it stopped her wondering what keeping him informed was likely to entail. 'What about Miss Killingley? Is she going to be sacked?'

'You really are a girl for introducing irrelevancies! Don't you think she should be?' he demanded in exasperation.

She sighed. 'I suppose you'd find it hard to trust her now.'

'Give me strength!' He leapt to his feet as if unable to contain his impatience. 'All right, I'll keep her on—for the time being—if you agree to sign that contract.'

This was the crunch, no more time for prevari-

cating. 'Will your lawyers handle it, or shall I put Mr
Forster on to it?' she asked calmly.

His face split into a grin that severely rocked her
composure. 'I'll get my man to draw it up then Mr
Forster can look it over before you sign. Just to make
sure I'm not doing you down,' he added mischie-
vously. He held out his hand. 'Shall we seal the deal
in the usual way?'

He was standing several feet away and even when
she got to her feet, made no attempt to move closer.
It was she who had to move to him, and as he took
her hand, instead of merely shaking it he used her
own momentum to pull her into his arms. Startled,
she began to protest, which was just what he had been
waiting for. His head swooped and his mouth captured
her parted lips.

Had he been brutal or forceful she might have
fought him off, but his kiss was gentle, so seducingly
sweet she found herself responding, and all too brief
so that when it ended she felt bereft.

No man had made her feel like this, not since Max,
and that it was just such another man as Max that
was having this effect on her now made it important
that he shouldn't know it. Gathering the rags of her
composure round her, she said mockingly, 'The *usual*
way? I can't see you sealing your agreement with
Simon Smylik with a kiss.'

'Simon isn't as pretty as you and anyway, his
boyfriend would have blacked my eye,' he retorted
wickedly. 'And you *did* say you don't have a
boyfriend.'

Before she could think up a smart answer he was
briskly businesslike again, pressing the intercom and
rattling out instructions to his secretary. 'Alison, get
Hywel Rees for me will you? And then ask Bainbridge
to be in my office in say . . . half an hour to draw
up a contract.'

While he waited for the call he said, 'The sooner

you meet Hywel, the better. Things haven't been running too smoothly so far.'

'Won't he mind me taking over half-way through?' Sorrel asked.

Before he could reply the phone buzzed and Luc snatched it up. 'Hywel? You'll be glad to know Eve Killingley is dropping out of the proceedings and the original designer is taking over.' He listened to a lengthy diatribe, his grin widening. 'Her name's Sorrel Valentine . . . Oh, a real stunner. Hair the colour of a polished conker and the wickedest pair of sherry-brown eyes I've ever seen.' Sorrel blushed scarlet as he went on to describe her other 'assets' before he finished, 'Well, you'll see for yourself.' He put his hand over the mouthpiece. 'This afternoon OK for you, Sorrel?' She gave her strangled assent. 'What's that, Hywel? Sure she's here with me.' He laughed. 'And blushing very prettily. Right then, I'll bring her along this afternoon, with her own set of designs, too. I've an idea Eve tinkered with the copies we have, to their detriment.'

CHAPTER SEVEN

TAMMY was ecstatic when she heard Sorrel's news, and once again tried to make her over for her meeting with the Welsh designer, but this time, bearing in mind that kiss, Sorrel was adamant.

'But this man's a *fashion* designer,' Tammy protested. 'Of *course* he's going to notice your clothes.'

In the end she compromised by wearing the chic woollen suit she'd worn for her interview with her father, and rather more of her jewellery than she would normally have worn at any one time. It wasn't until she went to her desk to get her portfolio of designs that she remembered she had locked them in and given Luc the key.

'Well, he'll be here in a few minutes,' Tammy pointed out when Sorrel began to panic.

'But suppose he doesn't have the key on him?' She rattled the drawer ineffectively.

Shaking her head, Tammy disappeared and came back moments later with Charlie, who eyed the lock and with a piece of bent wire and a few pokes and twists, slid the drawer open. 'One of the things I learned in my misspent youth,' he grinned.

It occurred to Sorrel that it might be useful if she took the few pieces of the range that she'd already made up, so she hurtled down to her workshop to take them from the safe let into the concrete floor. And only Sorrel knew that her uncharacteristic nervousness was due, not to the prospect of meeting the fashion designer, but to anticipation spiced with excitement at the expectation of seeing Luc again.

So her disappointment, when she went down to the doorbell's summons and found not Luc but his girlfriend Bianca beaming at her, was acute. She managed to cover it, jeering at herself as she got into the little sports car. Hadn't she already determined to restrict their dealings to business? So why had she allowed the memory of that kiss to make her forget? A man like Luc kissed easily, and sending his girlfriend to collect her had probably been deliberate.

To confirm her in that belief Bianca said excitedly, 'Luc told me what happened this morning when he took me to lunch. Oh, he sends his apologies, by the way, for not collecting you himself, but something came up. I was astounded when I heard what Eve had done. Mind you, I can't say I ever hit it off with her. It was pretty decent of you though, not to demand her instant dismissal. *I* would have done.' She giggled. 'But then I'm not as nice-natured as you. Still, I'm *delighted* the way things have turned out. It means we'll see quite a lot of each other.'

'We will?' Sorrel said faintly as the other girl paused for breath.

'Oh, yes. I modelled for Hywel last season and this range he's actually building round me. Well, me and Sara. She's blonde, you see, and with me being dark, we're a good contrast.' Pausing only to zip the car through a space Sorrel was sure was too narrow, Bianca burbled on, 'You've never met Hywel, have you? He's a dish. Very Celtic and excitable. You'll love him. No, I take that back because I rather fancy him myself. *He* didn't care for Eve, either. Of course, his place it just *chaos,* with Hywel screaming that he'll never be ready. But the launch is still seven weeks away and he *always* panics before a showing.'

Bianca flashed Sorrel a glance. 'You're looking pole-axed. I'm talking too much, aren't I?'

'N-no . . . ' Sorrel said faintly as the little car veered before Bianca righted it. 'It's just that every time you open your mouth I expect to hear a luscious Italian accent, not perfect English.'

Bianca laughed delightedly. 'Both my parents were of Italian origin but I was born and raised in England. In fact I'd never been to Italy until Luc took me last year, to meet some distant cousins.'

It was said casually, but it stressed again the close relationship the girl had with Luc, a serious one if he had taken her to Italy to meet her family. So what business did he have kissing her—Sorrel—only that morning? Since her student days Sorrel had taken great care to avoid situations where she would mind what any man did, and she was furious with herself for minding now.

Luc was waiting for them in a mews just off Bond Street. 'I got away earlier than I thought,' he said to Bianca, then, as Sorrel climbed out of the car on shaky legs, 'Sorry to subject you to this madcap's driving once again. I had more than a few qualms that she'd get you here in one piece.'

'Oh, you . . . ' Bianca thumped him playfully. 'I've had this car three months now and there's not a scratch on it.'

'Ah, but what about the other poor blighters, the ones that have to dodge out of your way?' One arm around Bianca's shoulders and the other around Sorrel's, he shepherded them through a glass door and pushed them ahead of him up a flight of stairs.

At the top, through another glass door, Sorrel glimpsed a large work-room, but Bianca was already starting up another flight. Here the corridor was darker and the door solid wood, but when Bianca pushed it open, Sorrel blinked in the sudden glare, for the entire ceiling was made of glass to let in the clear daylight.

The man studying the fit of the gown worn by a tall, willowy, silvery-haired blonde was far removed from the effeminate fashion designer of Sorrel's expectations. Stocky rather than artistically slim and the same height as Bianca in her very high heels, his brown, wildly disordered hair, greenish hazel eyes and square, pugnacious chin betrayed his Celtic origins. Indeed, in his cord jeans and bulky sweater he seemed to bring the wildness of his mountain homeland into this London studio.

'Luc, *darling!*' The blonde model was the first to notice their entrance and her rather bored face lit up.

'My God! You're not only late but you have to drag *him* with you.' The soft Welsh lilt didn't take the edge off the sarcastic accusation thrown at Bianca. 'Now I won't get another stroke of work out of this silly bitch.' He glared at the blonde who was fluttering her eyelashes at Luc.

'Don't be an old bear, Hywel.' Bianca didn't seem in the least put out by her reception. 'You knew very well Luc was coming this afternoon, and I'm late because I had to collect the lady responsible for those fabulous jewellery designs.' She nudged Sorrel forward. 'Sorrel Valentine—Hywel Rees.'

'Mr Rees.' Sorrel held out her hand and became the target of Hywel's green-eyed scrutiny.

'Hywel, please.' Still holding her hand he grinned widely at the man standing behind her. 'You're right, Luc, she *is* a stunner. And I see what you mean about those eyes . . . '

Sorrel's colour rose in the way she abhorred, and Bianca said sharply, 'I thought you were in a panic to get on, Hywel,' for the first time displaying a flash of jealousy Sorrel guessed was caused by learning of the appreciative remarks Luc had made about her.

Luc merely raised one eyebrow at her snappish tone. 'Sorrel's brought the original versions of her designs, Hywel, before Eve got at them.'

Hywel swept several swatches of fabric from the end of a long table. 'Let's have a look, then.' Taking the portfolio, he spread the drawings out. After only a few moments he demanded explosively. 'Why in hell didn't you show me these right at the start?'

Luc slanted a wry glance at Sorrel. 'It's a long story, Hywel.'

The designer grunted, his gaze pinning Sorrel to the spot. 'At least she has the virtue of silence, which has to be a plus after Eve.'

'Don't be misled. Sorrel can keep her end up all right.' Luc's teasing mockery and the reminder of their verbal sparring sent a shiver of excitement along her nerves which took a deep breath to control. 'I've kept silent because I've always worked alone before, Mr Rees,' she said coolly, 'And I'm uncertain what's expected of me.'

Hywel shot a surprised look at Luc who explained, 'Sorrel lacks Eve's experience in the demands of production, but I thought that drawback would be compensated by the ideas you would spark off each other.'

'Hywel . . .' The blonde made a bid for attention. 'Have you finished with me now? Only you know I have another appointment . . . ' She looked hopefully at Luc.

'How the hell I'm expected to have the collection ready on time when you girls are always elsewhere . . . ' the Welshman grumbled. 'All right, if you must. Molly . . . ' He addressed the fitter already helping the blonde out of her gown. 'Number twelve is ready for fitting, isn't it? The green? Get Bianca into it.'

While he unlocked a wall safe and took out a portfolio larger than Sorrel's, the two models unconcernedly stripped off to their undies, the blonde to don her own clothes, Bianca to wait while the fitter fetched a dress from the rack at the side of the room.

Pushing the fabric swatches even further down the littered bench, Hywel spread out his designs and motioned Sorrel across. Silently she scrutinised each page, her astonishment and excitement mounting. While still very modern, all the clothes had that slightly medieval flavour she had aimed at in her jewellery, with long, smooth lines, high waists and flowing sleeves. 'It's amazing!' She reached for one of her necklace designs, matching it with a smoothly fitting, high-waisted, low-necked gown where all the decoration had been concentrated into the sweeping sleeves. 'I mean, that we should both have been thinking along the same lines!'

Hywel laughed. 'While I'd like to pretend there was some mystical communion between us, I have to confess it was Bianca showing me your designs that gave me the inspiration. Trouble was, Eve kept trying to change things. It's marvellous to get back to the originals. Why on earth did you let her get at them in the first place?'

'At the time I didn't have any option,' Sorrel said drily with a sideways glance at Luc. But then she caught sight of the dress Bianca was now wearing, pale green but in a fabric with the sheen of a pearl; cut again on medieval lines, high-busted, long-bodied to flare from the knees with the fullness at the back, but with a wide, slit neckline reaching to the points of her shoulders and this time with long, close-fitting sleeves.

It was a beautiful dress and she saw at once how her jewellery could embellish it. Diving into her capacious shoulder-bag she brought out a chamois leather pouch, tipping the contents on to the table-top.

'You've actually got some of the pieces made up!' Hywel exclaimed.

'These were just try-outs.' She selected a long string made up of jade lozenges set in gold filigree. 'I only thought of this as a necklace but . . . ' She slung it round Bianca's waist, letting it sit on her hip-bones and hang low at the front.

'Oh, yes . . . ' Hywel breathed, viewing it from several angles.

'It'll need lengthening, of course, and the colour's not right,' Sorrel said. 'But it shouldn't be too difficult to find a deeper shade of green, and the matt texture of the jade shows up well on that lustrous fabric.'

Hywel gave a whoop. 'The girl's even prepared to compromise!' he exulted to Luc, whose presence Sorrel had momentarily forgotten.

Luc's smile was indulgent. 'Didn't I say you would spark each other's ideas? Well, I'll leave you to it. You can tell me how you get on when you have dinner with me tonight, Sorrel.'

Sorrel gaped at him, thinking he must have meant Bianca, but he was looking at her as if expecting an answer. 'Oh, but——' she floundered, acutely embarrassed, looking involuntarily at Bianca.

It was Hywel who came to her rescue, suggesting, 'Why don't we make it a foursome?'

'Oh yes!' Bianca suddenly came to life, wheedling, 'Please . . . Luc?'

The fact that Luc had issued his invitation in Bianca's hearing and now Bianca was pleading to be included, only increased Sorrel's embarrassment, as did Luc's resigned 'Oh, very well. Le Château, Hywel? I'll make the booking.' So when he went on to add, 'I'll pick you up at eight, Sorrel,' she refused firmly, telling him she would prefer to take a cab.

It took several minutes after he had gone to regain her composure, but once Hywel had taken her round his work-room and shown her the progress of his Collection, she was able to forget everything but which pieces of jewellery would go with which dress, and how other pieces might be adapted. Indeed, they were both so engrossed that when the cab deposited her back at Wapping, she had very little time to bath, dress and return to the West End. Ordering a minicab while her bath ran, she decided to wear the black silk suit Tammy had bullied her into for her first, disastrous interview with Luc, only this time teaming it with a fine black georgette blouse with a flounced neckline.

Wearing all black, she realised she needed a slightly more dramatic make-up, and regretted there wasn't time to arrange her hair in a more sophisticated style. As it was she was pushing her feet into high-heeled black sandals when the downstairs bell rang. Expecting it to be the minicab she didn't trouble to answer the entry-phone but grabbed her small black purse, checked she had her keys and sufficient money, and ran.

Breathless after hurtling down three flights of stairs, she stared at Luc and protested, 'B-but I've ordered a cab!'

'I know, I've just paid him off.' And when Sorrel began to splutter her indignation, 'I told you I'd collect you, and I have.' Tucking her hand under his arm he led her to his car.

The traffic was almost as heavy as it had been that morning, and after the second snarl-up Luc remarked, 'It looks as if we're going to be late, and all because of your silly scruples.'

Sorrel, who had decided a dignified silence was her best defence was provoked into snapping, 'Yes, I *do* have scruples, especially about hurting someone I like. How must Bianca have felt when she heard you ask me to dinner?'

'What gives you the impression she would be hurt?' he asked silkily.

Now he was making her feel as if she had read too much into his invitation—and into that kiss she still couldn't quite forget. 'Because I've seen the two of you together, heard her talking about you. You obviously have a close and long-standing relationship. Naturally she would be hurt to—to——' she floundered.

'To know I wanted to see you alone tonight? To know I very much want to make love to you?' he finished for her, and Sorrel's whole body burned with heated blood.

'You shouldn't *say* that!' she protested in a strangled voice.

'Why not, when it's true?' He sighed. 'Yes, Bianca and I are close. We are in fact, very fond of each other. But neither of us is of a jealous disposition—at least not about each other. And I think you'll find she will have been very happy to have had Hywel to herself for a while.'

Luc might feel that way, Sorrel thought, but she very much doubted if Bianca did, not when she remembered that flash of jealousy when Luc had apparently been admiring herself. But she held her tongue.

Indeed Bianca *did* seem happy enough in Hywel's company when Sorrel and Luc eventually arrived at the restaurant. She greeted them gaily, teasing Luc about his lateness, throughout the evening displaying not the slightest suspicion of jealousy, bantering with both men as if enjoying playing one off against the other. Only when Sorrel and Hywel got caught up in an enthusiastic account of their afternoon's progress did she fall silent.

For rather too much of the evening, Sorrel found herself comparing the two men. Hywel was really quite handsome in a rugged kind of way, and yet it was to Luc her eyes were irresistibly drawn. She and Hywel had a great deal in common; they were both creative, shared a common enthusiasm for their work and had discovered themselves to be mutually stimulating. Yet it was Luc, whose complexities she didn't think she would ever understand—let alone trust—of whom she was galvanically aware, noticing the strength of his large hands, the way the dark hairs on his wrist curled around the gold band of his watch, her eyes drawn often to the width of his shoulders beneath his well fitting dark suit, fascinated by his smile, though pretending to look elsewhere when it was aimed in her direction. It was not an awareness she welcomed, but she didn't seem able to escape from it.

'Is Luc taking you home, Sorrel?' Hywel asked when they had finished the dinner Sorrel could hardly remember eating.

'Of course he is,' Luc answered for her, accepting the return of his credit card from the waiter. 'It's my party and I brought her, so I get to take her home.'

Seeing Bianca looking tense again, Sorrel had a flash of inspiration. 'Why don't you *all* come? You said you wanted to see my place, Bianca.'

It was a bit of a squash, the two girls coiled into the narrow back seat, and somehow, each time Sorrel looked up, it was to meet Luc's eyes in the driving-mirror, eyes that seemed to promise retribution. A suspicion that was borne out when they arrived in Wapping and he whispered as he helped her out, 'You won't always be able to avoid me, Sorrel.'

But after visiting his office the following morning to sign her contract in the presence of Mr Forster, Sorrel did manage to avoid Luc for more than a week, spending her time with Hywel in his work-rooms co-ordinating her jewellery range with his Collection, taking each finalised design to Amoroso's production manager with details of the changes she wanted and discussing the gemstones needed. Whether Luc was in his office during her visits she never enquired but, remembering one of the conditions of her contract was that she keep him informed, she knew it couldn't last.

It was late on the Thursday night of the second week while Sorrel sat up rechecking some specifica-tions, that the phone rang, and even before she answered it, she knew it would be Luc.

'Did I get you out of bed?' The gravelly voice

invested an intimacy into the question that closed Sorrel's throat and dried her mouth.

At last she managed to croak, 'N-no, I was working.'

'At *this* time of night? My dear girl, I don't expect you to run yourself into the ground.' She could almost hear him frowning. 'Well, tomorrow you'll be taking the day off.'

'But I can't possibly——' she began.

'Oh yes, you can, I've cleared it with Hywel,' he contradicted. 'I've got something else lined up for you tomorrow—an interview with Miriam Gee, fashion editor of Lady Fair. I'll collect you at ten-thirty, well rested and ready to smile for the camera.'

'The camera!' Sorrel squealed in dismay, but he had already hung up. Dash the man for always wrong-footing her!

Talking about her work was something she could cope with, but this sounded as if it was going to be a much more personal interview if she had to be photographed, and worrying about the kind of questions she might be asked and how much of her background she should divulge kept her awake till the early hours. So naturally she had overslept and when the entry-phone buzzed she was still completing her make-up. Pressing the button she asked Luc to come up, and leaving the front door open, hurried back to her bedroom to brush her hair. Her choice of clothes that might be suitable to be photographed for a smart women's magazine was severely limited, and she had finally chosen the greeny-bronze dress.

She was just descending her spiral staircase when Luc appeared through her hallway. His gaze slid over her from head to foot, warm and somehow possessive, and Sorrel's nerves tingled in response, a similar rush of possessive feeling taking hold of her so that she had to grip the handrail to stop herself rushing down into his arms.

She was horrified at herself, and bewildered, too.

She had never felt such a . . . *proprietorial* emotion
about any man before, or such a savage sense of
betrayal because this man would never grant exclusive
rights to her or any woman. If a small part of him
belonged to anyone, then it was to Bianca, whom he
was still seeing. Only yesterday the gossip columns
had featured them dancing in some nightspot, together
with the surprising information that it was Luc who
was providing the financial backing for Hywel Rees.

Some of her pain must have shown on her face, for
he stepped forward, his hand outstretched. 'Sorrel?
What's the matter?'

Getting a grip on herself she descended the rest of
the steps. 'What should be the matter? she asked
lightly, trying to avoid those outstretched hands by
stepping round him.

But he wouldn't let her escape. Gripping her
shoulders he turned her to face him. 'You feel it, don't
you? This . . . recognition between us. It was there
even the first time we met, when I thought you were
a devious little schemer.'

Recognition. Yes, that was exactly what it felt like,
as if there was the man who could fill all the empty
spaces in her soul. And yet, how could she believe
that his feelings in any way corresponded with her
own?

'You don't believe me.' For a few moments she had
been so disturbed her doubts were clear on her face.
But even as he spoke, the mask of mocking amusement slid smoothly back.

'The same . . . recognition you've already experienced with any number of women? I may be green
but I no longer believe in fairy stories.'

The only betrayal that her gibe had struck its mark
came in the tightening of his hands on her shoulders.
'I get the feeling you don't believe in very much at
all,' he said flatly. 'All right, that's disposed of me,
but what about your feelings? And before you try to

lie your way out of it, I saw your face as you were coming down the stairs.'

Behind her mocking mask Sorrel felt naked. 'Oh, I admit I find you attractive,' she said carelessly. 'The chemistry's strong.' It was a desecration of her true feelings to speak of them so slightingly, but better than laying herself open to this man's magic and finding it was fool's gold.

'And that's all it is? Chemistry?' he pressed softly.

'What else?' she derided. 'You're surely not going to pretend you fell in love with me on sight?'

She watched the beautifully chiselled mouth tighten, knowing that if she hadn't started this argument he would be kissing her by now. 'No, I never pretend,' he said. 'Which is more than I can say for you.' Then, abruptly turning her towards the door, 'Right, if you're ready?'

And as she locked the door and clattered down the stairs with him, she found herself wishing he *had* kissed her, wishing he *had* tried to pretend, if only for a little while. Which only went to show how illogical and inconsistent she was, she silently derided.

Sorrel had no idea where the editorial offices of Lady Fair were, so she wasn't really surprised when Luc drew up at a parking-meter in a side-street off Knightsbridge. What did surprise her was when he hurried her into a smart boutique and demanded of the assistant, 'Is Magda about?'

'This isn't a magazine office,' Sorrel said as the girl hurried off.

'Full marks for observation! But it *is* a necessary preliminary to launching Sorrel Valentine on an unsuspecting world.' He turned away as a tiny redhead emerged from the back of the shop and flung herself into his arms.

'Luc . . . darling . . . ' She pulled his head down and kissed him lingeringly.

Sorrel looked away, shocked by the almost overwhelming urge to physically tear the two apart. It was one thing, she found, to know second-hand of Luc's reputation. It was quite another to actually see him with one of his women!

CHAPTER EIGHT

'THAT will teach you not to come to my party,' the prettily accented voice said playfully. 'Now, you may introduce me to your friend.'

Luc was grinning broadly as he obliged. 'Sorrel Valentine—Lady Magda Pendine. This wicked lady is very much married to a friend of mine,' he went on with pointed mockery as if he had read Sorrel's thoughts a few moments ago, and she felt herself colouring.

'But, of course, the jewellery designer!' Magda said warmly, holding out her hand. 'And we will drop the "lady", please, among friends. Bianca, she explained to me, and all is ready.' Not letting go of Sorrel's hand she drew her into a big fitting-room. 'Bianca described you well. I think you will like what I choose. You wait, Luc?' This she tossed over her shoulder.

'I wait,' Luc said.

As the curtain swished to Sorrel saw the rail packed with a wide range of clothes from casual wear to evening dresses, all, from their fabrics and cut, bearing designer labels and all patently expensive.

'You do realise that until a couple of minutes ago I had no idea I was buying clothes?' she complained. 'I could have on ragged underwear for all *he* knows.'

'Aah . . . you are not yet lovers, then?' Magda inquired interestedly.

Sorrel was taken aback and Magda shrugged dainty shoulders. 'If you were, you would not talk of ragged underwear.'

'No, we're not, and never likely to be,' Sorrel said crossly.

The mobile eyebrows rose, then Magda chuckled. 'I think you tease me, but anyway, I have plenty lingerie.' She lifted the lid of a box and while Sorrel goggled at the delectable froth of silk and lace, Magda slid down her zip and her dress slithered around her ankles.

For the next hour Sorrel climbed in and out of more clothes than she could remember seeing in her life before, and each one had to be modelled in front of an appreciative Luc. His final choice lay in a cotton jump-suit of two shades of clear, zinging orange that made her legs look as if they began beneath her armpits, a sage green dress with a pencil-slim skirt and blouson top in the softest suede and two evening dresses, one stark black and clinging, high at the neck but with no back to speak of and the other more romantic, low-necked and clinging lovingly to her breasts before skimming straight down to her feet, suggesting rather than revealing, and in a subtle blend of colours from palest lilac to deepest purple. There was nothing she could quarrel with in his choice—they were all beautiful and admittedly did something for her—but she resented that it was *he* who was making the choice.

To make her position perfectly clear she said to Magda in Luc's hearing, 'Right, if you'll just make out my bill . . . ' and was thankful she was carrying her credit card with her.

'Oh, but surely—Luc——' Magda looked helplessly at the man who had obviously given her other instructions.

'It *is* legitimate business expense, Sorrel,' he pointed out.

'Yes, to promote *my* business for *my* benefit,' she insisted stubbornly.

Inclining his head in acquiescence he said, 'Make out the lady's bill, Magda,' waiting until they got outside before admonishing, 'Independence is all very well, but it can be carried too far. I instigated this shopping spree and naturally I expected to pay for it.'

'And confirm Magda's suspicions?' She released her breath on a sharp sigh. 'Look, you know and I know I'm not your latest bed-mate, but rumours like that can hurt other people. Bianca, for instance.' She watched a frown put a deep crease between his brows and went on lightly, 'Don't look so worried, Luc. Although I don't usually indulge myself so extravagantly with clothes, it isn't going to make me bankrupt.'

Luc opened the boot of his car and tossed her packages inside. 'So I've discovered.' He laughed ruefully. 'I was way off-beam, wasn't I, suspecting you of trying to mend the family fortunes by a bit of confidence trickery? But I didn't know then—and you didn't tell me even later—that the godmother you spoke of was your father's cousin, Elinor Valentine, or that you inherited not only her considerable fortune but also her thirty per cent share in Valentine & Co! When I think about it! You've been a major shareholder since you were nine years old—equal to Marcia—and yet they've both ignored you. Haven't you played *any* part in the running of the firm? Been to a shareholders' meeting?'

Sorrel shrugged. 'My father held my proxy during my minority, and Mr Forster has acted for me since I came of age. And anyway . . . ' She turned on him angrily. 'How do you know all this?'

'I made it my business to find out,' he said imperturbably.

'Oh lord!' Sorrel bit her lip. 'Was it easy to uncover?'

'It wasn't hard. Why?' He looked at her curiously. 'It's not some deep, dark secret, is it?'

'As a matter of fact, it is.' Still biting her lip she looked at him doubtfully, but as he knew so much already, perhaps it would be safer to fill in the whole picture. She sighed. 'You see none of the others at the craft centre know I'm . . . well off.'

Luc's eyebrows climbed steeply. 'They don't? Why not?'

'Because I—we're a community.' She struggled to find the right words. 'They think I'm a struggling craftsman just like themselves. If they knew, it might—almost certainly would—make a difference to the way they see me and I wouldn't be one of them any more. You see, they're sort of . . . my family. So I would be very grateful if you would treat it as confidential information,' she finished in a rush, looking at him pleadingly.

His face looked as if it was carved from teak. Only his eyes showed any movement, a kind of deep, slow burn, and it was several seconds before Sorrel recognised it as anger, though she couldn't imagine what she had said or done to cause it. He didn't explain, merely saying tightly, 'You have my word none of them will learn anything from me.'

'Thank you.' She moved to the passenger door, waiting for him to unlock it, but he took her arm, turning her away. 'Not yet.'

Still tight-lipped and silent, he hurried her along Knightsbridge before turning into another side-street and pausing before a well known hairdressing establishment. 'An appointment's been made for you here.' He looked at his watch. 'I'll be back in an hour,' adding as he pushed her through the door, 'If I'm delayed, wait!'

Resentful of that last dictatorial instruction she gave her name to the receptionist who passed her on to a slender young man who introduced himself as Kris with a K. 'Bianca insisted I saw you myself,' he said, seating her before a mirror. 'Mmm, she was right; beautifully thick and in pretty good condition, but darling, no style!' He ran his hands through her hair, tumbling it in all directions.

Bianca had obviously been busy on her behalf, Sorrel thought as a junior shampooed her and, back once again before the mirror, she looked apprehensively at the scissors Kris was wielding, wincing when russet-brown locks began to fall. However by the time he had finished there was still enough hair to put up if she wished, but it felt indescribably lighter, settling back into place even when she shook her head, the new shape seeming to throw her cheekbones into greater prominence and make her eyes look larger.

She was paying her bill, adding a generous tip for the wizard who had effected the miraculous change in her appearance, when Luc arrived. Whatever he had found to do while he waited, his earlier anger seemed forgotten, the dark eyes smiling in open admiration.

'Just time for lunch,' he announced, sweeping her out into the car to lose all sense of direction in the byways of Belgravia, eventually halting near an establishment that announced its presence only be a discreet plate beside a discreet door. 'I hope you like Italian food,' Luc said, his gaze running over her slender figure. 'At least you don't have to fear pasta putting on inches.'

'As a matter of fact,' Sorrel confessed with a gleam of humour, 'Apart from opening the odd can of spaghetti, I've never had any.'

The horrified exclamations of both Luc and the hovering Italian proprietor made her grin widely, and as she was seated and the menu thrust into her hands, she was advised from two directions what she should sample. Laughingly she left the selection to them, and was not disappointed. From the crisp antipasto, through the *Zuppa alla Foubonne* to the *Pollo al Vino Bianco*, all washed down with a smooth Italian wine with an unpronounceable name, it was a feast both for the eyes and the taste-buds.

'You've made a convert, Tonio,' she laughed as he tried to press on her chestnut fritters as a dessert, 'But I couldn't eat another scrap.'

'You must bring her again, Luc,' Tonio said. 'Preferably for dinner. Is good to see someone enjoy my food.'

'Indeed I must,' Luc agreed, the way he was looking at her bringing a glow of colour to her cheeks. It wasn't

difficult to see why so many women jumped at the
chance of his company, Sorrel thought wryly, caught
once again in the spell of his wildly attractive sexual
charisma. This lunch with him had been . . . fun.

Full of good food and wine, she didn't at first notice
they were heading back towards Wapping. When it
finally dawned on her, she asked in rather sleepy bewilderment, 'What about this interview with Lady Fair,
then?'

'All in good time.' He grinned at her. 'I wanted to
relax you first, loosen up your inhibitions. And you'll
want to change into one of your new outfits, won't
you?'

'Oh lord!' Sorrel was suddenly remembering her
worries over how much of her background she should
reveal to her interviewer and wishing she had never
drunk all that wine.

'You have half an hour,' he said when he had followed
her into her apartment. 'They'll be here at three o'clock.'

'Here!' She stared at him. 'They're coming *here?* Why
didn't you tell me? The place is a mess . . . '

'Nonsense.' His reply was brisk. 'You're not the type
to live in a mess. This place looks exactly what it is, the
kind of place a creative artist can feel comfortable.
Miriam will be ecstatic. Now go and change.' He pushed
her towards the staircase. 'And wear the suede dress.'

There didn't seem much point in arguing, but as
Sorrel had her foot on the first stair she changed course
for the bathroom. If she was to undress, she would feel
safer with a locked door between them.

A quick sponge down and she shook the suede dress
from its tissue wrappings, loving the feel as its softness
caressed her skin. Touching up her make-up and
renewing her perfume from the small spray in her
handbag, she was as ready as she would ever be.

'They're on their way up,' Luc informed her as she
stepped nervously out of the bathroom. Almost
immediately her doorbell pealed, and while Sorrel was

still riveted to the spot, he went to answer it.

'Luc, *darling* . . . ' a feminine voice cooed, and although the light in her hallway wasn't good, Sorrel saw a pair of arms coil round Luc's neck to pull his mouth down. And this time, though his body blocked out the woman in his arms, Sorrel forced herself to watch, because if she ever allowed herself to succumb to the fierce attraction he exerted over her, this was what she would have to suffer, time and time again, until he tired of having her in his life.

Then Luc was turning, urging the visitor forward. She was of medium height, with brown hair, long and straight, falling girlishly almost to her waist, and yet as she came forward into the light, the girlish illusion was shattered, for this was a mature woman of perhaps forty, attractive rather than beautiful, her face lively with intelligence.

Luc performed the introductions and included the man ambling along after them, encumbered by cameras. 'So this is your little protégée, darling.' Miriam Gee looked Sorrel up and down knowingly before turning her attention to the apartment and calling excitedly to the photographer, 'Oh, Steve, you'll get some great pictures here. Just look at those windows!'

As she dragged the hapless Steve out of earshot Sorrel murmured to Luc, 'I thought you told me your intimate friends called you Luc.'

He smiled at her, slightly puzzled. 'And so they do.'

But Sorrel shook her head firmly. 'Oh no, your friends call you Luc. Your *intimate* friends call you Luc, darling.' She cooed the last two words.

He chuckled, his arm sliding around her shoulders. 'And when are *you* going to call me Luc, darling?'

'Oh, I don't see us ever getting that intimate,' she retorted smartly.

She was sure he was going to retaliate, but Miriam pre-empted him by saying tartly, 'You can flirt with her in your own time, Luc, not in mine. We'll do the photographs first, Steve has to get off.'

For the next hour Sorrel had her treasured privacy well and truly violated. Miriam prowled everywhere, even up into her gallery bedroom, and Sorrel was photographed in her small, neat kitchen, standing beside her tall windows, sitting at ease on one of her sofas; she was instructed to change into the bright orange jump-suit to be photographed working at her drawing-board, changed once again into the clinging black evening dress to be photographed at her dressing-table in her bedroom putting on some of her own jewellery, only to be hustled back into the jump-suit to be photographed downstairs at her work-bench.

It was almost a relief to see the photographer go off and to return to the apartment, but it was then the real questioning started. It was easy enough talking about her training and the kind of work she had been doing since setting up her workshop at Wapping. It was when Miriam asked what had prompted her to go into jewellery design that she hesitated.

Hesitated too long, for to her horror she heard Luc say, 'It was in her blood I should think, seeing that her father is one of the country's leading gem dealers.'

'Her father?' Miriam's head snapped up. 'Valentine. You mean *Felix* Valentine?' As Luc nodded, her gaze swung back to Sorrel, a look of stunned amazement on her face. 'Marcia Valentine is your *mother?*'

'No . . .' The denial came out like a strangled cry as she shot a look of bitter reproach at Luc. Marcia was never going to forgive her for this, and that meant her father wouldn't either. But now Luc had let the secret out, there was nothing for it but to put the record straight. Gaining control of her voice she said quietly, 'No, I'm his daughter by a previous marriage, when he and my mother were very young.'

Miriam pounced again, and Sorrel found herself answering questions about her mother and the Berisford-Reid family, fatalistically praying that they weren't going to be upset. At last Miriam was packing away her tape recorder and notebook, a gloating expression on her face as she said, 'You promised me a good story, Luc, darling, but I never dreamed it would be as good as this.'

When she was gone, Sorrel turned on him. 'How *could* you, Luc? I thought you were my father's friend! He's going to be very upset about this—not to mention Marcia.'

'Why the hell should he be upset? You're his daughter, for God's sake! A daughter any parent should be proud of; not only beautiful but highly talented.' He gripped her shoulders hard, reinforcing his argument. 'It's neither just nor reasonable that you should be hidden away as if you were something to be ashamed of, and I've already told Felix so. All right, so Marcia will have to bite the bullet for a while, but she'll get used to the idea.' His lips curled cynically. 'Knowing her, I guarantee within three months she'll be taking credit for your success.'

A lump had been rising in her throat while he spoke. He was taking her part—and against his friend! No one had ever shouted in her corner before, and that Luc should be doing so now touched her deeply. Her mouth working as she tried to master her emotion, she asked huskily, 'You told my father?'

The hard anger in his eyes softened to something like tenderness while his grip on her shoulders gentled to a caress. 'Yes, I told him, and he agreed with me.' He watched her disbelief warring with a terrible yearning as tears welled in the wide, sherry-brown eyes, and he was struck by how like the face that was lifted to him now was to the face behind the mask in that extraordinary portrait he had seen in her bedroom, and he knew a stab of unreasoning jealousy that the painter, too, had seen below the surface to the real, very vulnerable woman he held in his arms.

'He did?' she asked wonderingly, and he found himself

wanting to reassure her, to give her everything she
lacked. He pulled her against him, his senses leaping at
the contact, but experience told him this was not the
time to indulge the desire licking like fire through his
veins, and he turned the embrace into one of comfort.

'Yes, he did, and to prove it, he and Marcia are
having dinner with us tonight.'

Sorrel's eyes widened incredulously. 'In public?'

'At the Savoy, and you can't get more public than
that. So put your feet up for an hour, then have a long,
leisurely bath——' he had to clamp down on a sudden
surge of desire '—and glam yourself up in that pretty
lilac evening dress. I'll be back to collect you at eight.'
He kissed her gently and very sweetly, and she was so
stunned she responded blindly.

By the time she was walking beside Luc through the
portals of the famous hotel, Sorrel was shivering and
stiff with nerves. 'It's all very well for you,' she said
when he teased her, 'but I've never even been inside a
place like this before.' Suppose she did something gauche
and made her father ashamed of her, she worried
silently.

'I guarantee there won't be a lady there I'd be more
proud to be seen with.' His encouraging words were
accompanied by the warmly reassuring clasp of his hand
as he led her through the foyer. She was still looking
up at him idiotically as they walked into one of the bars
where her father and Marcia waited.

The evening turned out to be less of an ordeal than
she had feared. Conversation was a little stilted at first,
especially with Marcia, but under Luc's skilful direction
even she thawed, until by the end of the evening she
was openly introducing Sorrel as her stepdaughter to
friends who paused at their table, ignoring their astonishment and implying that only loyalty to her mother
had kept Sorrel away from her father's family for so

long. Sorrel exchanged wry amusement with Luc, but her father's open pleasure in her company more than made up for his wife's face-saving fiction.

Not until the two ladies adjourned to the powder-room did some of Marcia's true feelings surface, when she said tartly, 'I do hope you're not going to make a fool of yourself over Luc, my dear. It can be pretty heady having a man like him paying you attention, but don't forget that he and Bianca Fratelli have been a regular number for some time.'

'If you're warning me not to fall in love with him,' Sorrel retorted coolly, 'there's no need. Even if it weren't for Bianca, I have more sense than to fall for a man who has women standing in line for him.' They were brave words but very hollow, because after what he had done for her tonight, she was already more than half in love with him.

'It wasn't so bad, was it?' Luc said as they waved Felix and Marcia off.

'You know it wasn't.' Her father had just invited her to his home to meet her two brothers during their next holiday from university and her voice was husky with emotion as she looked up at him. 'I—thank you, Luc. Without you it wouldn't have been possible.'

He put a hand beneath her chin and kissed her lightly but with exquisite tenderness. His own voice was slightly husky as he teased, 'Now don't go mushy on me. *They* may be going home but for us the night's only just begun.'

She sniffed, managed a shaky smile and admonished, 'Luc . . . it was very good of you to arrange this dinner with my father, but——'

'It wasn't good of me at all,' he broke in, 'and it isn't good of me to take you on to a nightclub either. In the first place, I would very much like to dance with you, and in the second place, now we've cleared things with your father and Marcia, it's time to get the gossip columnists talking about you.'

'Gossip columnists!' She stared at him in horror.

'Not a breed I admire, but I learned early that if they were going to use me, there was nothing to stop me using them.' He flagged down a cruising cab.

She was still staring at him in bemused bewilderment after he had given the driver the name of a nightclub she had only ever read about. 'I haven't the slightest idea what you're getting at.' She lurched against him as the cab swerved out into the flow of traffic.

'It's simple.' His arm snaked round her to steady her. 'Just a matter of dropping the right word into the right ear at the right time. So when I want a bit of free publicity I make sure I'm photographed partying with some beautiful lady, and I just "happen" to mention whatever it is either I or the lady want to make known. That's how we launched Magda Pendine's boutique, and Hywel's first Collection, among other things.'

'You partied with Hywel!'

'No, idiot, with Bianca and the other models he was using at the opening.'

If what he was implying was true, it gave an entirely different slant to his so-called reputation, the many photographs she had seen in the press of Luc escorting one beautiful woman after another. 'So it'll just be a publicity exercise,' she said, and though it might square her conscience regarding Bianca, it also brought a sharp stab of disappointment.

'That's right,' Luc agreed, reading her disappointment and taking encouragement from it. 'Tonight we're promoting the newest star on the jewellery design scene. You *did* agree to make yourself available for any necessary publicity,' he added wickedly.

The club had the reputation of being capriciously selective in the patrons it allowed through its doors, but Luc's arrival was warmly welcomed. Their progress to their table was lengthy as Luc was greeted by so many people, and to each group he introduced Sorrel as the find of the century, warning them not to miss the launch of her fabulous jewellery designs, puffing her up so much that even people she recognised as household names were looking at her as if she was someone special.

When they finally reached their table he ordered champagne and laughed at the expression on her face. 'What's the matter, darling? Don't you like being a celebrity?'

That casual 'darling' acted like a supercharger to her pulse rate, and she found herself wishing with a terrible yearning that she *was* his darling. 'I feel as if I've been hit by a ten-ton truck,' she said ruefully, and he would never know how true that was.

They danced and talked, all the time being interrupted by people who wanted to talk to Luc, sometimes women who cooed and pawed him with covetous hands, sometimes men who leered at Sorrel knowingly, and once by a smooth gentleman who asked pertinent questions and whom Luc revealed, after he had moved on, as the gossip columnist on a popular daily paper.

Feeling like someone who had jumped in at the deep end, Sorrel let the waters close over her head, giving herself up to the seducing movements of his body against hers as they danced again. So what if it was all a publicity stunt? For just a short time she could pretend she was in his arms because he wanted her there. No past, no future, no commitments elsewhere, tonight he was hers, and when they left here they would go back to her apartment . . . Her body caught fire at the voluptuous pictures her imagination was conjuring.

It was at that moment a flash bulb popped in her face and the dream shattered. Luc smiled down into her dazzled eyes. 'Mission accomplished, I think. We might as well leave now.' Moments later they were out on the pavement and he was hailing a cab, giving the driver her Wapping address.

'What about your car?' she questioned half-heartedly, for suddenly she was feeling cold and very tired.

He assured her he would collect it later, and when he

asked the driver to wait while he escorted her to her
door, she didn't know whether to be relieved or disappointed. 'You're nearly out on your feet, darling.' He
kissed her gently and pushed her inside. 'I'll call you.'

She very much doubted it. Hadn't he said, 'Mission
accomplished?' But call her he did. Half a dozen times
during the next two weeks they spent a similar evening
together, being seen at all the places the wealthy and
influential disported themselves.

When that first photograph was published, it had
seemed to Sorrel that her feelings for the man whose
arms held her must be blazingly obvious, but though
she watched closely for Bianca's reaction, she could
discern no change in the girl's friendly attitude. It only
confirmed her certainty that Luc had been telling the
truth when he asserted his reputation in the gossip
columns had been deliberately sought for publicity
purposes, and that Bianca was sure enough of his
feelings for her not to worry.

Only once did the model appear to get uptight, when
the third photograph came out and Hywel teased, 'You
do realise the whole of London believes you're lovers?
But at least you don't look quite so starry-eyed this
time.'

Aware that Bianca was within hearing, and surprised
and cross at his insensitivity, she retorted, 'Whatever
London believes, the people who matter *know* it's only
a publicity stunt.'

'Oh, good. There's still hope for me, then.' Hywel
shot an oddly taunting glance at Bianca and the look
she returned was definitely hurt.

The conviction that Luc's consistently amorous
behaviour was only a ploy to build up public interest in
the launch of her jewellery designs made it easier for
her to combat it, though when he kissed her the voice
of reason was difficult to hear over the clamour of her
senses.

It was on their sixth 'date' that things changed. To

begin with it was no 'in' place he took her to, but a quiet restaurant where the tables were discreetly widely spaced and the postage-stamp-sized dance-floor encouraged closeness. No one greeted them as they threaded their way to their table, or interrupted them as they worked leisurely through the menu, yet Luc was even more attentive and lover-like.

Being full of the delicious *veal hongroise,* Sorrel declined dessert, only to find the aroma of Luc's *crêpes* drenched in Cointreau titillating her taste buds. Smiling at the childlike longing of her expression, he scooped up a portion and popped it into her mouth.

It was a subtly erotic experience, being fed from his plate with the same fork he was using, and a trembling began inside her. 'There are no reporters watching our act tonight,' she said shakily in an attempt to get her feet back on firm ground.

'No, there aren't, and that's deliberate.' Something seemed to flare in the dark depths of his eyes. 'I decided I'd let you back off long enough. Tonight is for us.' He pushed his plate aside and took her hand. 'Come on, let's dance.'

Weakly she allowed him to lead her on to the floor, though once there, what they participated in was not like any dancing Sorrel had known before. With his eyes and his hands and his body he was subtly making love to her to music. And caught in the thrall of his enchantment, she found herself sinking without a struggle, her body taking light from his, her senses sending to her brain only messages of sheer, intoxicated delight. Her arms coiled submissively around his neck, her fingertips exploring the texture of his hair, the skin above his collar, and longed to explore further. Her body arched closer to his as his hand caressed her back, bared by the slinky black dress, her mouth tasting the skin of his jaw while his ragged breath stirred the hair at her temples.

After twenty minutes of this exquisite torture, the

tension between them spiralling higher and higher, he suddenly groaned in her ear, 'For pity's sake, let's get out of here!'

With indecent haste he paid the bill and almost dragged her out to the car. But nothing seemed to break through her enthralment as she took little sideways peeks at his strangely set face. Only when the car surprisingly swooped down into an underground car park did her bemused brain try to send out warnings.

'Where are we?' she asked as he hustled her out of the car and across to a lift.

'Home,' he said shortly, pushing her into the small compartment, and before the doors had closed she was being gathered into strong arms and the electrical charge was re-ignited, short-circuiting her mental processes. The evidence of his powerful arousal brought a shivering, heated excitement surging through her nervous system, a response her already weakened defences had no hope of withstanding. Arms tightening round her, his breathing fast and suddenly ragged, Luc traced her delicate jawline and when he reached her mouth, she went up like tinder, opening to his deepening kiss, her arms winding round his neck to draw him closer with a driving need. Nothing existed but the strength of his arms holding her ever tighter, the mind-blowing, ecstatic sensations of his mouth and tongue against hers as he tasted, explored, reaching into her to draw her very soul from her body.

It was some time before either of them realised the lift had stopped and the doors were now open. They drew apart reluctantly and Sorrel gazed up at him with dazed, uncomprehending eyes. No longer the cool, well groomed playboy, his bow-tie was crooked, his dark hair falling across his brow while a faint mist of perspiration beaded his upper lip. 'Wait . . . wait . . . ' he said feverishly, hurrying her out of the lift and across to a door. His handprint on a metal plate opened it and he pulled her inside.

About to take her in his arms again like a starving man, a discreet cough had both their heads turning. 'I shan't need you again tonight, Peter.' Luc's voice was harshly impatient.

'Very well, sir. Goodnight.' The man silently withdrew but his brief presence acted on Sorrel like a douche of cold water.

'This is your home?' She looked round the enormous entrance hall, a rug she recognised as Chinese glowing with jewel colours against a polished parquet floor, and she counted six doors leading off before Luc ushered her through one of them into the kind of sitting-room she had only seen in expensive magazines. Huge and softly lit, its understated elegance very modern—curtains at the wide window that looked like silk tweed, an even larger Chinese rug as the centrepiece of a conversation area, pictures on the walls that were surely originals—it was the home of a rich man accustomed to getting what he wanted.

'Why have you brought me here?' she asked, knowing the question was naïve from the way he smiled.

'Because you're driving me crazy, and I couldn't wait until I got you back to Wapping,' he said frankly, moving to draw her back into his arms. But she evaded him. Maybe the deliberate courting of publicity *had* been behind all those ladies he had been reported partying with, but that didn't mean to say he hadn't made love to them.

'To get me into your bed,' she said flatly.

'To make love to you,' he corrected. 'Sorrel, I've made no secret of how much I want you. And a moment ago you wanted me too, so don't deny it.' He caught her and kissed her devouringly, and the word want . . . want . . . want . . . echoed round her brain.

Yes, she did want him, in all the empty, ravening places in her soul, but she wanted—*needed*—more than that.

CHAPTER NINE

AT LAST Sorrel's lack of response got through to Luc. 'You're fending me off again,' he accused and, thrusting her away, he crossed to a bar where he poured himself a generous whisky. After a long swallow he said wearily, 'Hell, I didn't mean to put the pressure on till after the launch, but maybe my tactics have been off-beam from the start. I shouldn't have let you off the hook that night we dined with your father. I could have taken you then.'

And he might have succeeded too, for that was the night when she had first recognised that what she felt for him was more than sexual attraction. But the words he used, 'tactics', 'put on the pressure', 'want', 'take', they weren't the words of love. 'I'm—I'm sorry if—if my behaviour misled you.' It was hard to speak for the ache in her throat. 'But you—you're an experienced man, and I . . . What I'm trying to say is . . . I don't sleep around.'

There was an electric silence and then he clipped out, 'I'm delighted to hear it but, though I may not be a virgin, neither do I.' And then with a strange, almost eager expression on his face he said, 'Is *that* it? Sorrel, are you a virgin?'

Her cheeks burned with embarrassment and there was an element of resentment, too. As far as Luc was concerned, that could be the only acceptable reason for her turning him down. 'No, I'm not.' This evening had coaxed her out from behind her usual mask of amused mockery, but now it slid easily into place, hiding emotions too vulnerable to be put on show. 'It's because

I'm *not* a virgin that I know casual sex isn't for me.'

Luc's face was expressionless, only his eyes burned. 'So, who was he? Someone who meant a lot to you?'

He had no right to ask, but telling him might reinforce her defences. 'A man very much like you,' she mocked. 'Very attractive, very charismatic, but, like you, he preferred variety to commitment. Oh, my friends warned me he tried out all the new girl students, but at eighteen I was too green to know there was a difference between desire and love. I was in love and thought he loved me, too. I thought moving in with him was a mere preliminary to marriage and living happily ever after. Two months later he was asking me to move out to make way for my successor.'

Luc was staring down into his drink. 'And that has been your only relationship with a man?'

'No, then there was Trevor.' She laughed, mocking herself. 'Oh, by then I was much more cautious, and Trevor was a very different type, a fellow student, serious, and he wanted to marry me.' She laughed again. 'You see, I'd very foolishly told him my father was Felix Valentine of Valentine & Co, gem dealers. When he discovered I wasn't even on visiting terms with my father, and that marrying Felix Valentine's daughter wouldn't give him a boost up the career ladder, he suddenly found all sorts of reasons for calling the engagement off.'

In the years since, Sorrel had come to realise that her own particular vulnerability had been to blame for all that heartache and disillusion. She could recognise now that her desperate need to be loved and to love in return was a legacy of her unloved, unwanted childhood. But although she was older and wiser now, she knew she was no more fitted for the light, careless love affairs a lot of her generation indulged in than she had been then. Maybe marriage and a family were not the crock of gold at the end of the rainbow, but she needed the kind of commitment that would assure her she was loved, and that was something Luc couldn't give her.

Silently Luc put down his glass and came to stand in front of her, tipping her chin so he could see her face. 'Yes, the mask is very firmly in place again. But I got behind it for a while tonight, and I'll do it again. Come on, I'll take you home.'

When they were in the car, he suddenly asked, 'Who painted that portrait of you? The one in your bedroom?'

'Ch-Charlie,' she said, disconcerted.

Risking a sidelong glance she saw his brows rise. 'Has he exhibited?'

'Not unless you count the railings along Green Park,' she said ruefully.

They talked of Charlie's work and Sorrel's assessment of it until they reached Wapping, where he escorted her to her door, unlocking it before kissing her with great deliberation. 'That,' he said, his thumbs lightly smoothing the blue bruises beneath her eyes, 'is a declaration of intent. Wriggle all you like, Sorrel, but you and I are going to be lovers.'

Four days later, Sorrel was still as taut as a harpstring, jumping whenever the telephone rang. The launch was less than three weeks away now, and all her jewellery designs had been finalised so the necessity of working closely with Hywel was over. It didn't help her peace of mind that she was having to visit the Amoroso publicity department to help them with the press releases, but although Luc must have known when she was on the premises, not once did he try to see her.

She told herself she was relieved he had apparently thought better of his threat and had ceased his pursuit, but all too often, mostly in the dark reaches of the night, the hunger he had awoken in her kept her awake, his promise that they would be lovers circling her brain. And she wondered whether she hadn't been a fool to turn him down. Maybe he couldn't give her the love and commitment she craved, but wouldn't it have been something to carry in her memory down the long, empty years? He had been honest with her, admitting that he couldn't pretend he had fallen in love with her, but she loved him, so for her it would be more than a self-indulgent gratification of the senses. And wouldn't even a brief affair with him have been better than nothing?

And when he inevitably tired of her and moved on? Would she be able to bear the anguish of watching him walk away? But by then—the thought hit her with stunning force—by then he might have left her with something just as precious as his love. She lay trembling as she thought of bearing Luc's child, a unique being created by their—her love. A human being that would be entirely dependent on her, someone to love who would return that love unconditionally. The child would have to grow up without a father's guidance and influence, but then she'd had to do that herself, and at least *her* child would have the compensation of a mother's love. And she had so much to give a child. Unlike most women faced with single parenthood, she would have no financial worries. She wouldn't have to ask Luc for support. In fact, he needn't necessarily know. She didn't *have* to stay in London. She could work anywhere, a cottage in the country perhaps, somewhere with plenty of room for a growing child to play, like Ellie's house in Kent. That had been sold many years ago, of course, but there must be many similar places where money was no object. Her imagination was already picturing it, a rambling garden with secret places for a small, dark-haired boy to explore . . .

The sound of a police car ululating through the night brought her back to cold reality. She had turned Luc down so she had missed her chance. And anyway, there was Bianca. Over the weeks her liking for Bianca had grown and the feeling was mutual, their friendship becoming the kind of relationship Sorrel would have liked to have had with her sister. And Bianca loved Luc, that was something else these last few weeks had underlined, even if he sometimes treated her like an

indulged child. How would she be able to face Bianca
if she and Luc became lovers? The vision of the dark-
haired, dark-eyed little boy faded and Sorrel shivered,
cold and alone.

Once more the telephone rang, drying her mouth and
turning her knees to jelly, but there was a distinctive
Welsh lilt to the voice which said, 'Sorrel, can you get
over here this afternoon?'

Pretending the hollow feeling where her stomach
should be was not disappointment, she agreed she could,
although he refused to tell her why he needed her. An
hour later she discovered what he had deemed so
important as Molly, his head fitter, helped her out of
her jeans and sweat shirt and into a half finished dress
in cream cotton, the front pin-tucked in a complicated
diamond pattern so it fitted closely over her high bust
and dipped down to a pointed stomacher in front where
the cleverly cut skirt clung lovingly to her hips before
swirling about her knees, the long sleeves pleated and
full on the shoulders but narrowing to fit closely from
the elbows and ending in a point over her wrists.

It was a beautiful dress but Sorrel protested, 'Why fit
it on me, Hywel? You're not expecting *me* to do any
modelling!'

'Don't look so panic-stricken,' Hywel soothed. 'This
is exclusive to you to wear at the launch. My present
for being such a honey to work with.'

'You've made it for *me!* Oh, Hywel . . . ' She was
so touched a lump as big as a bucket stuck in her
throat. 'I don't know what to say . . . how to thank
you.'

As if embarrassed by her emotion, he grinned.
'Couldn't have you turn up wearing some other designer's creation, could I? Wouldn't do my image much
good if the customers thought the star didn't fancy my
clothes.'

'I'm not the star,' she remonstrated, 'and I love your
clothes. That velvet suit, for instance . . . ' Hywel had

achieved the medieval theme on a modern skirt and jacket with the clever use of two toning shades of brown velvet, and Sorrel had hung her nose over it ever since she had first seen it. 'I'm thinking of putting in an order.'

'An order for what?' Bianca's bubbly voice had a smile curving Sorrel's mouth before she turned her head, but when she saw Luc standing in the doorway behind her, the smile died. 'I haven't seen that before!' Bianca was staring at the dress Hywel was still fitting, an uncertain frown drawing her dark brows together. 'I thought Sara and I were doing all the modelling.'

'Yes, I thought he'd gone mad for a few minutes. But it's all right,' Sorrel laughingly explained, 'apparently this is what I'll be wearing on the day. Isn't it gorgeous? So generous of Hywel.'

All the time she had been talking she had tried not to look at Luc, but irresistibly her eyes were drawn in his direction to be held in his hotly possessive stare. 'That's right,' he said deliberately. 'I asked Hywel to design something special for Sorrel.'

It had been *Luc's* idea! Not for anything could she bring herself to look at Bianca.

'I think that's it then, Sorrel.' It was the first time Hywel had spoken since the other couple had arrived. 'And if you're sure you can spare me some of your time . . . ' he turned to Bianca, his voice dripping sarcasm.

'As long as she can be ready when I pick her up at five,' Luc answered for her, and to Sorrel's surprise, Hywel bristled at him like a dog whose territory was threatened.

'I'll be ready, Luc.' Bianca's dark eyes seemed to be pleading with him to go, and after the door had closed behind him, she said placatingly to Hywel, 'It's just a business appointment, Hywel, like this afternoon. As a matter of fact I've found a flat, one I don't have to share, and Luc's helping me out——'

'I'm not interested in the arrangements for your love life,' Hywel cut her off curtly. 'Molly . . . ' he turned to the fitter. 'Get her into that red dress . . . '

While the subdued Bianca did as she was told, he asked Sorrel what jewellery she would wear with the cream dress, and almost on the same breath they both suggested a matching set of ear-rings and necklace in graduated opals.

'You see how well tuned we are?' Hywel said. 'Why don't we discover what else we share thoughts about over dinner tonight?'

Trying to forget the powerful possessiveness in the way Luc had looked at her, and to prove to Bianca she had no designs on her man, Sorrel agreed.

For all his claim that they were so closely tuned, Sorrel found him preoccupied, almost morose that evening. She introduced several topics of conversation with little response, until he suddenly said, 'This new flat of Bianca's . . . do you reckon Amory's setting her up?'

Ever since Bianca had mentioned the flat, Sorrel had been keeping that same suspicion at bay. Now Hywel had put it into words she had to face the distinct possibility, face out and ride the pain that possibility brought. Bianca sharing with other girls must have cramped Luc's style, it was only natural he would prefer more privacy when they were together. The only wonder was that he hadn't set her up in her own flat before this. Or perhaps Bianca had held out against it, hoping he would marry her? Anyway, if he had finally persuaded her to his way of thinking, it would explain why he had suddenly dropped his pursuit of Sorrel herself.

'It's highly likely,' she said, trying to sound indifferent. 'They *are* very close. I mean, you only have to see them together to know——'

'Then why doesn't he marry her?' Hywel demanded with angry vehemence. 'Spoiling her life, that's what he's doing. Keeping her on a string, jerking her back to

him when it suits him, leaving her dangling when he
decides to pursue someone else. If he doesn't want her,
then why doesn't he let her make something of her life
with someone else?'

The Welsh accent had become more pronounced
under the strength of his feelings and Sorrel found
herself regarding the young fashion designer with a new
sympathy. 'You're in love with her, aren't you?'

Thick, stubby lashes swept down over stormy hazel
eyes and a flush stained his cheekbones. 'Am I that
bloody obvious?'

'Not obvious at all, in fact the penny's only just
dropped.' Or maybe she had been too blinded by her
own unrequited love to notice Hywel's. If only Bianca
had returned his feelings! It wouldn't have made all
Sorrel's dreams come true but at least she could have
settled for an affair with Luc with an easy conscience.

Remembering the enthusiastic way Bianca had spoken
about Hywel when they had first met, Sorrel said
diffidently, 'She does like you, Hywel. She once told me
you were very dishy and as good as warned me off.'

'Like me?' he said morosely. 'Yes, she's given me to
understand there's a green light showing.' His eyes
hardened and his hands clenched round his glass. 'But
hell! I don't just want a tumble in the hay. I want to
marry the girl!'

Sorrel was struck by a shaft of envy. To have a man
like Hywel offering so much, and to turn it down . . .
And then the envy died and was replaced by understanding as she put herself in the other girl's place. As
attractive as Hywel was, could she herself have accepted
him, knowing how she felt about Luc?

The waiter came then to show them to their table,
and it wasn't until after they had ordered that Sorrel
asked, 'Does Bianca *know* you want to marry her?'
Perhaps if she did, she thought hopefully . . .

'Do me a favour!' Hywel killed her hopes stone dead.
'I may be a boy up from the valleys but I'm not daft.

Just because Luc doesn't want her enough to offer her a wedding ring doesn't mean he'd take kindly to me doing it. How do you think I'd stand with him if she told him I was trying? He's financing me, don't forget, and it'll be years before I pay off the debt.'

Sorrel had forgotten. 'So you'd run the risk of not only losing the girl but your business as well.'

'Got it in one.' Hywel pushed his bowl of soup away hardly tasted. 'I did hope for a while . . . ' He hesitated, then plunged on, 'Well, you were seeing a lot of him, and I saw the way he looked at you, as if he wanted to eat you . . . ?' He broke off questioningly and Sorrel's cheeks burned.

'I told you, that was just publicity,' she protested, hoping the blush wouldn't give away how much further than a publicity stunt it had gone.

'Yes,' he said heavily after the waiter had cleared away their plates. 'Though I wouldn't put it past Luc to take advantage of the situation.' He hunched his shoulders, adding explosively, 'You'd think Bianca would have more pride! I mean, she knows about all the other women he sees. She's even seen the way he looks at you.'

Sorrel put her knife and fork down abruptly. 'She—she's seen?' She swallowed down a lump of guilt. 'What—did she say anything?'

'Oh yes, that in that case I shouldn't have any scruples about taking her out.' He stabbed the steak on his plate as if he wanted to kill it. 'But if she thinks I'm going to play second string to Luc Amory, let her use me to bring him to heel . . . '

Sorrel was horrified to realise that not only had Bianca noticed Luc's pursuit of herself but she had actually discussed it with Hywel. 'Was she—upset?'

'Bloody angry,' Hywel revealed, and Sorrel winced. 'Anyway, the question's academic if they're going to be virtually living together,' he finished.

They were both busy with their thoughts, only toying

with their food, until Sorrel gave up the effort and
Hywel signalled the waiter. Both of them declined
dessert and settled for coffee, but before it could be
brought there was a slight commotion and they both
looked up to see Luc bearing down on them with a set
face and Bianca following in his wake.

Without ceremony Luc pulled the astonished Sorrel
to her feet. 'Bianca wants to talk to Hywel,' he said,
pushing the girl into the vacated chair and marching
out with Sorrel dangling from his wrist like a dog on a
leash.

'Luc, what on earth are you playing at?' Out on the
pavement Sorrel managed to get him to stop, but only
because he was opening the door of the Mercedes to
push her inside. 'Luc . . . ' She tried again as he took
the seat beside her. 'Look, you can't *do* this. Bianca
looked terribly upset when you left her in there.'

'Of course she was upset, you stupid bitch,' he snarled,
and in the face of his incomprehensible anger she shrank
away. Slamming the car into gear he pulled away with
a screech of tyres. 'She had to listen while her man
made a date with you, see you just now mooning over
him while he sweet-talked you. And she's not the only
one who's upset.'

Sorrel stared at him, shaking her head in bewilderment. 'I don't know what you're talking about. I've
made it very clear to her that all my dates with you
were a publicity——'

'God, how can a supposedly intelligent woman be so
thick!' he said rudely. 'It's Hywel we're talking about.
Hywel, that fancy Welshman. He's the man Bianca
wants, not me. God, I've tried hinting, even tried telling
you point-blank that Bianca and I don't have any kind
of romantic attachment. Now will you shut up and let
me drive?'

Sorrel bit her tongue on all the questions she was
burning to ask. Indeed, all her energies were needed
holding on to the edge of her seat as Luc made for

Wapping at a speed that made her expect to hear the
wail of a police car at any moment.

Luc's face was still livid with rage as he manacled her
wrist and dragged her to her door, snatching the key
from her and marching her up the stairs.

As he pushed her into the apartment she made haste
to put some distance between them, only turning to face
him once she was behind the comparative safety of the
largest sofa. 'Now perhaps you'll tell me what's eating
you and stop behaving like a madman,' she said bravely.

'If I am mad, it's you who's responsible,' he ground
out, advancing on her. 'What do you mean by dating
Hywel? You're mine, I told you that days ago. I will
not have you making it with other men.'

'I was not!' she began indignantly. 'We were having
dinner, for heaven's sake!' She edged round the other
end of the sofa, alarmed now as well as bewildered.
'Please Luc . . . sit down and let's talk about this
sensibly . . . '

But he still kept coming. 'Oh no, a little retribution's
called for after all you've put me through these last few
weeks, never mind tonight. We'll talk, but not until I've
kissed you senseless.'

There was an undignified scuffle as she tried a last-
minute swerve to elude him before finding herself in the
coils of a boa constrictor, her mouth being plundered
ferociously. But although it might have started out as
punishment, her traitorous body's instant response had
the hard demand of his kiss softening to supplication.
'Now I've got you where I want you, you blind . . .
prejudiced . . .   blinkered . . .   infuriating . . .
stupid . . . ' Each word was punctuated by a kiss as
his mouth blindly explored her face and neck.

' . . . thick . . . puzzled . . . bewildered . . . '
she added for him, punctuating with her own kisses.

' . . . fascinating . . . bewitching . . . addictive
little darling,' he finished.

They were words she wanted to hear from Luc,

wanted to hear so much she was in danger of actually believing them. 'Luc . . . ' She managed to get her hands between them to hold him a little away. 'Luc, will you please explain that extraordinary statement you made in the car. About Bianca and—and Hywel?'

'What's to explain, for pity's sake?' he groaned, only reluctantly abandoning his exploration of the whorls and curves of her ear with his tongue that was making it impossible for her to think. 'If you hadn't been so ready to listen to gossip and to leap to all the wrong conclusions, you'd have noticed for yourself that it's Hywel Bianca wants. She's been nuts about him since she worked for him last season, and she thought she was making headway until you came along.'

'Me? But . . . ' Sorrel shook her head, trying to clear it. 'Hywel only asked me out tonight because you and Bianca——' She suddenly remembered the reason for Hywel's despondency. 'If Bianca loves Hywel, then why is she setting up a flat with you?'

'With me? What in thunder gave you that idea? I have a perfectly good home of my own.'

'But—but you went with her to look at the flat, and to see about the lease. Bianca said so.'

'And your nasty little mind immediately had us shacking up together.' He shook her, not altogether gently.

'Well, everyone knows how close the two of you are,' she defended, her hair flying in all directions. 'And if I didn't have eyes enough myself, everyone's been telling me so, even my stepmother . . . '

'And you listened to them, rather than me!' To her relief he let her go, running his hands through his own hair in frustration. 'Yes, I took Bianca under my wing more than a year ago, and though I care about her, I am *not* sleeping with her—nor do I intend to. Look, if I tell you that before he died, Bianca's father made me her trustee . . . *now* do you see why I was helping her arrange her new flat? I had to be there to authorise the release of her funds to buy the lease.'

'Is that the truth?' All the longing to believe him was there in her eyes for him to see.

'It's the gospel truth,' he declared gravely. 'And if Hywel asked you out tonight to get back at Bianca, why did you accept, darling? Dare I believe it was to punish me?'

Sorrel could find nothing to say, though the colour staining her cheeks was admission enough. He groaned, drawing her back into his arms. 'I told you you were mine, and I meant it. I also promised we would be lovers, and I don't intend to wait any longer.'

A shudder shook her as desire flared like a forest fire before the wind. Why not? her mind was demanding, even as her body clamoured for the fulfilment only this man could give. Hands and mouth and eyes caressed her as he slid down her zip and coaxed the fragile chiffon from her shoulders, hands that explored the silky skin, mouth that tasted, eyes that worshipped. And Sorrel's hands and mouth and eyes were making their own exploration, easing off his jacket until it dropped to the floor, touching the bunched muscles beneath his shirt until even that wasn't enough. It was his hands that tore off his tie, but hers that scrabbled frantically at the buttons of his shirt, fingertips delighting in the tactile pleasure of warm, slightly moist, hair-roughened skin, fascinated and awed by the hard, powerful muscles as she ran her hands over his shoulders; pleasures she had hungered for, yet that faded into insignificance at the explosion of sensation as her hardened nipples touched his bare chest.

Luc's convulsive gasp told her he was similarly affected, and as his head plunged to taste the creamy mounds with their eager buds with lips and tongue, she arched against him, dissolving into mindless pleasure at the avid tug of his mouth. The room spun round her and she found herself horizontal on the sofa with Luc kneeling beside her. Hywel had commented on the way

Luc ate her with his eyes, and he was doing that now, as if what he was seeing was a feast to a starving man, his hands shaping what his eyes were seeing, testing the weight of her breasts in his palms, his thumbs brushing tormentingly over the aroused peaks, smoothing the curve of her waist and the flatness of her belly, caressing away her tights and panties, raising the heat inside her to an intolerable pitch.

'Please . . . oh please, Luc . . . ' Was that really her moaning and pleading for him to take her? She writhed beneath his tormenting hands, knowing only the driving need to have this man fill all the empty spaces in her.

'Gently, my darling, gently,' he murmured. 'I've waited too long to blow it now by being too impatient.' But his hands shook as he stood to rid himself of the rest of his clothing.

She watched, dry-mouthed, the rippling muscles of his arms and shoulders as he bent, the long, straight, muscular perfection of his legs, the narrowness of his hips, and she trembled at the evidence of his powerful arousal. Sitting up with the glazed eyes and raised arms of a sleep-walker, she touched him and felt him tremble, too.

And then he was lying beside her and she was revelling in the benediction of skin touching skin, legs entwined. She gave herself up to her exploration of this man, this other half of herself, all the fevered dreams and imaginings of weeks culminating in this incredible reality. And she responded to Luc's similar exploration with abandonment, discovering in herself a capacity for voluptuousness and sensuality she had never dreamed of.

Whispering endearments, telling her how beautiful she was, his hands and mouth plundered all the secret places of her body, teasing, delighting, arousing her to such a pitch she could stand his withholding of himself no longer. Legs twining round his, her hands cupping his neat buttocks, she pulled him into her fiercely, gasping aloud at his penetration, filled with wonder, elation and a deeply possessive joy at knowing him part of her at last. There was nothing . . . nothing in the world like this. This was what she had been born for, this deep satisfaction, the fulfilment.

And then, as with a groan he began to move inside her, she realised she had still only reached the foothills of fulfilment. With each slow, deep thrust she climbed a little higher. Inexperienced as she was, her own body moved instinctively to his rhythm in a communion that was as old as time and as new as an undiscovered star, until with an explosion of unimaginable pleasure the star burst into a million shining, scintillating fragments and she began the slow, weightless floating back to earth.

'My God!' His breath still gaspingly uneven, Luc sounded shaken. 'I suspected you were hiding passion beneath that cool cynicism of yours, but I never dreamed . . .'

She arrived back to earth with a bump, reminded that what for her had been the deepest expression of her love had for Luc been merely passion, enjoyable no doubt, but no different to the passion he had shared with many other women. What had seemed at the time to be a communion of body and spirit was now revealed as slightly seedy, merely the gratification of greedy senses on a sofa, with hastily discarded clothing littering the floor.

Luc was suffering no such disillusion. 'You wonderful, wonderful woman.' His arms still held her possessively as he buried his face against her neck. 'God, I don't think I'll ever have enough of you. Sorrel, will you let me stay tonight?'

Sorrel closed her eyes, longing to say yes, tempted beyond bearing to experience his devastating love-making once more. But already doubts about his true relationship with Bianca were re-animating in her mind.

She had allowed his claim that it was Hywel Bianca loved to persuade her into his arms because she had *wanted* to be persuaded, but she still wasn't convinced. Couldn't he have made that claim in order to get through her defences? He had openly boasted that one day they would be lovers and he wasn't a man who took kindly to being thwarted.

'Do you think that's a good idea?' Her voice was husky. 'Suppose Bianca tries to contact you tonight?'

'Then she'll find I'm not at home,' he said reasonably.

'Yes, but then she'll know where——' Sorrel licked her dry lips. 'She knows you brought me home, so she'll know you stayed and . . .'

He raised himself on one elbow, looking down at her frowningly. 'I thought I'd settled the question of Bianca. She's a dear girl but I have never been, and am never likely to be, romantically involved with her.'

Conscious of her nakedness Sorrel sat up, drawing her knees up and wrapping her arms around her legs so she felt less exposed. 'Maybe *you* feel like that, but . . .' She looked at him with troubled eyes. 'Hywel told me tonight that when he and Bianca discussed your attraction to me, she was *angry*. Well, she wouldn't be angry if she hadn't been jealous, would she? And she would hardly be jealous if she didn't feel more for you than she would if you were merely her trustee.'

'What an uncomfortable conscience you do have,' Luc said irritably, 'especially as I doubt if anyone's ever had a conscience over you. Why should it worry you *what* Bianca feels?'

'I'm sorry you find it uncomfortable,' she flashed back. 'But I care about Bianca. I have to work with her for several more weeks and I would have liked to keep her friendship for much longer. I've grown very fond of her. She—she's what I would have liked my sister to be.'

He sighed and stood up, then without a word and completely unselfconscious of his nakedness he walked to the bathroom, coming back a few moments later wearing her bathrobe. 'A man's robe?' he queried.

'The ladies' sizes are always too short for me. Luc——'

'You have another robe?' he interrupted.

'Yes, in my bedroom, but——' He was already climbing the spiral staircase and when he came down again he tossed a fleecy apricot-coloured robe to her. 'Put that on, this could take some time.'

While she scrambled into her robe he went over to the windows, drawing the curtain back and staring out into the night. 'The place Bianca has in my life has been a stumbling-block in quite a few of my relationships, but this is the first time it's mattered.'

Sorrel watched him, sensing a battle going on inside him, then as if making up his mind, he came back across the room to stand before her, his hands fondling her shoulders while his dark eyes seemed to search her brain. 'I want you to promise me that what I tell you now will never go beyond these four walls,' he said.

CHAPTER TEN

SOMETHING in Luc's voice, the way his dark gaze held hers, convinced Sorrel that this was something important to him, and she nodded. 'Anything told me in confidence . . . you don't need to ask.'

'No, I don't think I do,' he said softly. 'You of all people should understand . . . ' His hands slid down her arms to her hands, drawing her back to the sofa where he settled into a corner pulling her against him. 'I don't know if you know it, but Amoroso is my family name. My grandparents were both born in Italy and only came to England when they were first married to open the London branch of the Amorcenti Galleries.'

Sorrel's head twisted round to look at him. 'I didn't know you owned Amorcenti, too!' It was a very famous art gallery just off Bond Street.

He smiled. 'My grandfather, Luciano Amoroso, and his cousin Paolo Viscenti were partners. The Viscenti line still runs the Italian operation but my grandparents prospered here, they liked London and settled. So my father was born and raised here, educated at an English public school and university. He saw himself as more English than Italian. His given name of Giovanni he changed as a schoolboy to John, and later anglicised his surname to Amory, much to my grandmother's disgust.' A faint smile curled his mouth. 'I can still remember her; she came from a patrician Venetian family and was very proud.

'As I went through the same educational system, I can see my father's point. Being English with a foreign name must have been a social drawback. His family had wealth and an excellent business reputation, but he wanted social acceptance too, and he achieved it when he married my mother, who was the youngest daughter of an Earl.'

Sorrel was finding all this of fascinating interest, though she couldn't see where it was leading, or what it had to do with her not wanting to hurt Bianca, but not for anything would she have interrupted.

'By that time my grandfather was dead and my father was running the English end of Amorcenti, and very successfully too, especially as he began to number 'old wealth' as well as the new among his clients. I don't suppose as a child I was particularly observant, but there was nothing to suggest my parents' marriage wasn't just as successful. I know my father was disappointed there were no more children, but he always seemed devoted to her.

'I don't know, maybe his Italian blood was stronger than he realised, but on one of his trips to Rome he met a young Italian woman and they fell in love. But he was a Catholic and divorce was impossible. Besides, what reason had my mother given him for deserting her? He might have married her for all the wrong reasons but she had been a good wife to him. So he brought the lady back to England and quietly installed her in a house in Highgate. And for years he lived a double life, visiting his mistress whenever he could.' The look of distaste on his face was marked and Sorrel wondered if this was why he was so against committing himself to any one woman—if, like his father, he was incapable of it.

The suspicion added another stone to the weight in her heart. 'Did you know about his . . . other woman?'

'Not until I was in my middle twenties, but about ten years ago my father suffered a slight stroke. It frightened him, made him realise how vulnerable his Gianetta was. He wanted to make provision for her without it showing up in his will and hurting my mother. So he took me into his confidence.'

Sorrel sensed what a shock it must have been and touched his hand sympathetically. He caught it and held it fast. 'Not only did he tell me about the woman he had loved for so long,' he said quietly, 'he told me too about her daughter, a little girl at school. Her daughter . . . and his.'

She stared at him, everything falling into place. 'Bianca!' she breathed.

He nodded. 'My father recovered and lived for another seven years, and after his death I took over as her guardian. Her mother's health was failing by then and I was all the family she had. So you see, my darling . . . ' he caressed the pure line of her jaw, 'there is no way you and I being together can hurt Bianca. Of course we love each other—but only as brother and sister.'

'And your mother still knows nothing?'

'And must *never* know,' he reiterated. 'She loved him right to the end. It would be too cruel to destroy her illusions now.'

Sorrel silently agreed. 'Thank you for telling me, Luc.' She felt immensely proud that he had trusted her with his confidence, proud and honoured that this secret only Bianca and Luc himself knew, he had now shared with her. What was it he had said, that the place Bianca had in his life had caused problems before, but with her it was the first time it had mattered? Surely that must mean *she* mattered to him? And not merely as a possible conquest? But it would be dangerous to follow that line of thinking to its logical conclusion. Hadn't he already told her he wasn't going to pretend he had fallen in love with her? She mustn't read too much into these confidences and start dreaming about a future.

Even so, she knew she wasn't going to allow the lack of a future to spoil the chance of embracing the present. As long as she kept it light . . .

'It's very late, Luc.' She watched his expectancy crumble and wondered if any other woman had succeeded in confusing him before. Smiling, she went on, 'Of course, you're very welcome to spend the night on my sofa. Personally, I'm going to bed . . . and I had rather hoped you'd want to come with me.'

With a growl he leapt to his feet, swinging her up into his arms. 'Tease . . . witch . . . temptress . . . ' He started for the spiral staircase and she squealed, clinging to his neck.

'Luc . . . no! You can't carry me up there, you'll break both our necks! And even if you get us up in one piece, you'll be no good to me when we get there.'

'Casting aspersions on my virility now, are you?' But he swung her down on to the lower stair and with his hand on her bottom, pushed her up in front of him at a rush while she giggled breathlessly, all her doubts and inhibitions firmly shelved. She would take each day at a time, grasp whatever happiness was offered and be thankful for it without yearning for the impossible. Time enough after he had gone to torture herself with the bleakness of her future without him.

Leaving only the bedside lamp burning, she plunged the rest of the apartment into darkness, flung back the duvet and, letting the robe slide from her shoulders, held out her arms to him. For the present he was hers, her lover. She would love and cherish and value him as no one had before or would again, and she would be happy for as long as it lasted.

It lasted just two and a half weeks. A magical time when every moment spent together was precious. Sorrel felt lit from within, glowing with health and crackling with energy in spite of the exhaustingly passionate nights. During that time they spent a couple of nights at Luc's St James's apartment, but because Sorrel was always conscious of Peter, the houseman who lived on the premises, most of their nights were spent at Wapping, where, after bursting in on them sharing breakfast that first morning, Tammy and Charlie had left them discreetly alone. There was still much to be done before the launch of her jewellery collection so they travelled together to the Amoroso building in the mornings, usually late because Luc was so reluctant to get out of bed, and she was only too eager to stay.

As Luc had forecast, Bianca was delighted for them. 'A publicity stunt!' she derided. 'I knew from the first you two were made for each other.' She sighed. 'P'raps when Hywel sees how happy you are together it will get it through his thick skull that dating me isn't going to upset his financial director.'

Unfortunately, Sorrel saw very little of Hywel in the increasingly fraught run-up to the launch, and never when she and Luc were together. There were last-minute hitches to be ironed out with the production manager, arrangements to be checked at the hotel where the joint showing was to be held, so when they did meet it was always at a moment of crisis. Neither was she able to judge whether Hywel's attitude to Bianca had changed. Stupidly, she decided to let the matter rest until after the launch.

The day dawned bright and sunny, a perfect May morning when, for once, they didn't dare linger in bed. On their way to Hatton Garden Sorrel reviewed aloud all the tasks she must find time for before the invited audience arrived.

'Excited?' Luc slanted her a smiling glance.

'Well, naturally, and nervous too. Suppose the buyers don't like my work?' It wasn't just the society women in the audience she had to please. Buyers from retail outlets worldwide who stocked Amoroso products would be there too, and that was where the real business lay.

'They'll snap it up,' Luc assured her confidently. 'I told you, Sorrel Valentine is going to be the new name in jewellery design.' He dropped a warm, caressing hand to her thigh. 'Just as long as you still love me when you're famous.'

Her senses instantly aroused by his touch, she let her eyes feast on him. She wanted to tell him she would love him till the end of time, but knew his playful comment wasn't expected to provoke such a serious answer. 'As if being famous would make any difference when you only have to look at me.' She could make the lightly self-mocking admission because he was already well aware that he could arouse her from across a busy room, and because she knew she had the same power over him—for the present.

The last minute checking and reminders were done from Luc's office, and then they collected the jewellery, saw it safely into the hands of the security guards and followed the armoured vehicle to the hotel.

It was chaos. Electricians were making last-minute adjustments to the lighting, florists were still adding finishing touches, carpenters still hammered at the catwalk and white-smocked men were putting out dozens of gilt-legged chairs. And behind the scenes even greater chaos reigned.

'It's just Hywel doing his temperamental Celt act,' Bianca sighed as she sat at a dressing-table in a thin robe finishing her make-up. 'Though he's not usually quite such a bastard.'

'You still haven't sorted things out between you, then?' Sorrel asked sympathetically and Bianca grinned.

'Anything but! I still can't seem to convince him Luc hasn't set me up in my new flat as a little love nest.'

'Perhaps when we all go out to celebrate tonight we'll be able to convince him,' Sorrel said hopefully.

It was time for her to change into the beautiful cream dress Hywel had designed for her, although during the actual showing she was going to remain behind the scenes to help the girls with their quick changes and to make sure they wore the right jewellery with each outfit.

The next hour or so passed in a blur of activity, the

excitement and elation rising each time the models came back to change into the next outfit and to report on the gasps of admiration and approval and the spontaneous bursts of applause.

And then it was time for the last ensemble, Sara and Bianca both wearing bridal gowns, pearl jewellery to suit the ethereal quality of the silver-fair Sara, while Bianca's dark hair and veil were held in place by a gold circlet studded with garnet cabochons, a late addition to the jewellery collection, as was the matching necklace and ear-rings.

The applause was thunderous, people at the back standing on their chairs as those at the front rose to their feet. Flushed and triumphant, Hywel went out on to the catwalk to join the girls and moments later Sorrel found herself being pushed out there too, at first stunned by the noise and the flash bulbs popping her face, but then relaxing and beginning to enjoy it when Luc sprang on to the catwalk to join her.

Waiters began to circulate with champagne. A glass was pushed into her hand as Luc helped her down on to the floor. 'Don't drink it too quickly,' he warned, smiling at her bemused expression. 'You'll need to keep your wits about you. Everyone will be clamouring to meet you.'

And it seemed he was right. Almost instantly they were surrounded and then split up. Her father was one of the first to congratulate her, hugging her and beaming proudly, and even Marcia unbent enough to brush her cheek and coo enough compliments to satisfy any bystander. It seemed to go on for ever, the congratulations and expressions of admiration, and by the time the crowd began to thin out, Sorrel had run out of new things to say in response.

'Quite a triumph, and thanks to darling Luc, my magazine is the first of the glossies to carry the story.' Sorrel identified the speaker as Miriam Gee, the fashion editor who had interviewed her.

'Yes, I still don't know what's hit me,' she admitted dazedly.

'I'm sure you don't.' There was a cat-like smirk on Miriam's face. 'Luc's a devastating lover, isn't he? Makes a girl feel really special. Pity it doesn't last.'

Sorrel gasped at her spite, feeling a shaft of bitter jealousy that this woman had also known the rapture of Luc's lovemaking. But before her stunned brain could formulate an answer, Miriam was saying, 'I don't suppose he's introduced you to his mother, has he? No, of course he wouldn't.' She didn't need to say a man didn't introduce his current mistress to his mother because Sorrel knew with a sick humiliation it was true.

'Let me do the honours for you.' With a hand clamped round Sorrel's wrist to prevent her escape, Miriam waved to attract the the attention of a very gracious-looking lady standing only a short distance away, dressed in the style the Queen Mother adopted, the well preserved complexion beneath the off-the-face hat impeccably made up.

Sorrel looked round frantically for Luc, and finally spotted him surrounded by a coterie of Japanese gentlemen, buyers, she guessed, not looking in her direction and too far away to notice what was going on.

And already it was too late. Miriam was saying silkily, 'Lady Anne, may I present the talented designer of all that lovely jewellery, Miss Sorrel Valentine.'

'Done in your best Debrett style, Miriam dear, but Mrs Amory has been good enough for me for the last forty years.' She turned smiling brown eyes on Sorrel. 'A most unusual collection of jewellery, Miss Valentine. I've just been taking a closer look at it.' The jewellery had been set out on display, suitably guarded, and had gathered an admiring crowd. 'It all makes me feel covetous, but there were a couple of pieces in particular I shall have to talk nicely to my son about.'

Sorrel murmured something appropriate, liking Mrs

Amory's natural friendliness and wishing she could be natural in return, but too conscious of her precarious position in Luc's life and afraid of causing him embarrassment to allow herself to respond to that feeling of rapport.

'And the clothes!' Mrs Amory enthused. 'Such a flattering line for a woman of any age. There's at least one I must order. I've been trying to find Mr Rees to tell him so, but——' she looked around helplessly. 'He seems to have disappeared.'

'I saw him going through there a few minutes ago.' Miriam Gee nodded towards the curtains behind the stage. 'With Bianca. They seemed,' she added with another of her cat-like smirks, 'to be arguing.'

Seizing the opportunity to escape from the invidious position into which Miriam had thrust her before Luc noticed, Sorrel said eagerly, 'Let me fetch him for you, Mrs Amory.' Without waiting for a reply she hurried away.

It wasn't until she was through the curtains that she realised Luc's mother had followed and was right behind her, and by then they could both hear the raised voices. 'Will you stop tormenting me, girl!' Hywel's accent was very Welsh under the pressure of his emotions. 'Do you think I have no sense of loyalty, Bianca? Luc Amory's done a lot for me, I'd never have got off the ground without his backing, so how can I do the dirty on him and take his woman?'

'For the hundredth time, I am *not* his woman,' Bianca shouted, tears thickening her voice. 'You may not have noticed but he's not seeing anyone but Sorrel just now.'

'So you're using me to make him jealous,' Hywel said contemptuously.

Sorrel's face flamed, knowing Luc's mother must have heard, and she turned abruptly to usher the woman away from these embarrassing revelations, but Mrs Amory seemed to have been struck to stone as Bianca sobbed, 'Jealous? How could he be jealous when he's my *brother!*'

· Sorrel saw the shock in the sagging mouth and widened eyes of the woman whose arm she had grasped, felt the muscles jerk beneath her fingers. Desperately she wished them both elsewhere, but the hidden voices went inexorably on.

'Your *brother!*' Hywel sounded as shocked as the two listening woman.

'Oh, God!' Bianca's voice caught on a sob. 'His—we had the same father . . . ' The admission was made much more quietly but still only too clearly. 'But you mustn't tell a soul. Promise me, Hywel. Luc'd never forgive me if it got to his mother's ears . . . '

Mrs Amory moaned, her face paper-white, the lines of age suddenly deeply etched as her body sagged. Sorrel was afraid she was going to faint and gathered her close to support her. 'Mrs Amory . . . ' Thankfully the quarrelling voices had fallen to an indistinct murmur but the damage was done. All Sorrel could think of was getting the older woman away before Bianca showed herself. 'Mrs Amory . . . ' she urged again, and at last the woman seemed to come out of her rigour of shock, whispering, 'It's not true. It *can't* be true!'

'No, of course not,' Sorrel tried to reassure her as she steered her to a side door that would lead them back to the main room without having to be exposed on the catwalk. The noise of chatter and laughter hit them like a blow and Mrs Amory flinched. 'Luc . . . ' she said pathetically, and suddenly he was there, taking in his mother's sagging figure and Sorrel's tense, worried face.

'What's the matter?' His glance seared her and she was sure he must be wondering at finding his mistress with his mother. But now wasn't the time for explanations.

'Your . . . Mrs Amory isn't feeling well,' she said inadequately, knowing the guilt she was feeling was emblazoned on her face.

'Mother?' His voice was sharp with concern

'It—I'll be——' Tears began to roll down the powdered cheeks. 'Take me home, Luc . . . please.'

'Yes, of course, darling.' He was frowning and darted another glance at Sorrel whose guilt made her feel it was full of condemnation. 'I'll see you later,' he said quietly, and she watched as he supported his mother from the room. She stood there, straight and slender and alone, once again knowing herself the outsider.

But no one else was aware that her moment of triumph had turned to dust and ashes, and mustn't know, she vowed as she called on all her pride to be polite to the people who were still coming up to speak to her.

Her father brought a man who wished for an introduction, Seth Dewis, an American who owned a rival jewellery house in New York, a man in his forties with predatory eyes and a cajoling tongue which he used to try to persuade her to come to New York and design for him.

While she was flattered at his persistence, she had to tell him she was under contract to design exclusively for Amoroso for the next two years. He still insisted he would make it worth her while to break her contract, but Sorrel was only half listening. It was an hour now since Luc had taken his mother home and he still had not returned. Was he very angry that she had the nerve to get herself introduced?

'Aren't you afraid that if I break my contract with Amoroso, I'll break it just as easily with you?' she asked the American sardonically, the worry about Luc still fretting the edges of her mind.

'I reckon I can keep you so happy, you won't want to,' Seth said confidently. 'My products outsell Amoroso by a long way in the States, and there could be other . . . inducements.' Those predatory eyes told her what those 'inducements' were, and Sorrel sighed.

Were all men alike? Like small boys seeing a toy they coveted, and grabbing?

She finally ceded him the promise that if she ever found herself in New York she would be in touch, and allowed him to press his business card on her, to which he had added the telephone number of his private apartment. It seemed the quickest way to get rid of him.

At last the society women, the buyers and the press all departed and Sorrel was overseeing the packing of her jewellery to be returned in the security van to Amoroso when she saw Hywel and Bianca approaching. Hand in hand, she noticed, and such a glow on Bianca's lovely face she knew at last all had come right for them. She shivered as she wondered at what cost. But she pushed the thought away and smiled at them. 'Your Collection was a stunning success, Hywel. Congratulations.'

'Double congratulations, Sorrel.' Bianca was brimming with happiness as she looked at the man at her side, revelling in the proud possessiveness of his return glance. 'Hywel's just asked me to marry him.' Tearing her eyes away from him she looked around the room. 'Where's Luc? I must tell him . . .'

'He—he had to take his mother home. She wasn't well.' Sorrel couldn't bring herself to dim their happiness by telling them their quarrel and Bianca's revelations had been overheard, let alone by whom.

'He's gone!' Bianca wailed in dismay. 'But he'll be coming to our celebration tonight?'

Sorrel rather doubted if Luc would be in the mood for celebrating. She only hoped that when his mother told him how she had learned of his half-sister's existence, it wouldn't damage his relationship with Bianca.

'I would think the only celebration you need tonight is strictly for two,' she said, managing to instil a teasing note into her voice. 'I really am very happy for you both.' She hugged Bianca and placed a friendly kiss on Hywel's cheek.

They didn't argue, still too wrapped up on the newness of their happiness to make more than a token protest when Sorrel insisted on taking a cab back to Wapping to wait for Luc.

Tammy and Charlie pounced on her before she could open the door, demanding to know how things had gone. Both had been given invitations but had turned them down on the practical pretext that Tammy would never be able to afford either the clothes or the jewellery and so should make space for those who could. Sorrel told them as she made tea and kicked off her high-heeled shoes to sit down and drink it, naturally leaving out the traumatic event that had cast such a blight.

Only when Tammy had extracted every detail did she lean back with a satisfied beam of suppressed excitement. 'Now we've got some news for *you*. Charlie, you tell her.'

Charlie shifted his great bulk and grinned sheepishly. 'We've 'ad a visitor, chap called . . . ' he looked questioningly at Tammy who supplied, 'Colin Armstrong,' then went on, 'Anyway, Luc asked 'im to take a gander at my work, and guess what?' Before he could supply the answer, Tammy, unable to hold back any longer, broke in, 'He's offered Charlie an exhibition, Sorrel!'

Caught up in their excitement, she shot upright. 'He has? But that's wonderful! Congratulations, Charlie. Your talent's being recognised at last. Where? When?'

'At the Amorcenti Gallery, of course,' Charlie said as if she ought to have know that. 'In nine months' time.'

The gallery Luc owned. Well, of course she should have known, as soon as Charlie had let slip that it was Luc who had asked this man to see his paintings. 'He never breathed a word about it, though I knew he was very impressed by those two paintings of yours that I have, Charlie,' she said, for just a few moments feeling a little hurt that he'd kept her in the dark, and then realising that this way Charlie would know the offer had been on the merit of his work and not because of her connection with the owner of the gallery. It was the kind of thoughtfulness that made her love him all the more.

After they had gone, Sorrel lay for a long time in a scented bath, wondering how long Luc would be, or even if he would be able to come at all tonight. Knowing from the way he had spoken about his father's extra-marital liaison that his sympathies lay with his mother, she resigned herself to the possibility that he might not be able to leave her if she was very upset.

Getting out of the bath she patted herself dry and slipped on her bathrobe, brushing out her hair and just touching her eyes with shadow and mascara and her mouth with lip gloss. Feeling very much a spare part and vulnerably lonely, she stood for a while at the high windows watching the life on the river before pulling herself together and making for the kitchen. The least she could do would be to have some sort of meal ready if he *did* come.

It was after ten o'clock and she was dozing on the sofa when at last the sound of his key in the lock had her swinging her feet groggily to the floor. 'Luc . . . ' The grim expression carved into his face brought back that damnable feeling of guilt. 'How—how is she?'

'Under sedation, as if you care!' he ground out savagely, then gripping her upper arms, 'Why? Why did you do it?'

She had expected him to be angry with her for her unwilling part in the events that had caused his mother such humiliation but she recoiled from the sheer savagery of this attack. Licking her dry lips she said guiltily, 'I know you would rather I hadn't spoken to your mother, Luc. I mean, that was obvious when you didn't intro-duce us, but——'

'Is that why you did it?' His eyes bored into her with angry incredulity. 'Because you thought I'd slighted you?' He flung her away from him as if he could no longer bear to touch her.

Stumbling to regain her balance, Sorrel looked at him in bewilderment. 'I—I didn't deliberately seek her out,' she defended herself, 'but Miriam Gee insisted on introducing us and——'

'And you couldn't wait to get back at me by betraying my confidence,' he finished for her in fierce disgust.

At last she began to realise just why he was so savagely angry. Obviously his mother had been in no state to explain exactly what had happened and he had jumped to the conclusion . . . Shaking her head in vehement denial she began, 'Luc, you *can't* believe that I——'

'Who else could have told her?' he snarled. 'I didn't, and Bianca certainly wouldn't. You were the only other person who knew. And you were still with her when I found her in a state of collapse.'

White-faced and stunned, Sorrel realised how bad it must have looked to him, and frantic denials were crowding her tongue, only to die unspoken as he went on with ice-cold savagery, 'My God, what a fool I was to trust you! And for what? To gain a few weeks' access to your delectable body.'

She had known, of course, right from the beginning, how ephemeral their relationship was, but his cruel words, his icy self-disgust drove the message home like nails striking into her heart. What for her had been the deepest expression of her love for him had been nothing more than a passing pleasure, something that could be had from any woman.

Everything that was in her wanted to cry out, to tell him he was wrong, that his accusations were unjust, but even if he believed her, what good would it do? The happiness she had cherished, believing in spite of everything that it had the value of pure gold, had shown itself for what it was, fool's gold, shining briefly like the real thing but crumbling and worthless.

As she was worthless to Luc, merely his mistress, to be enjoyed while his passion lasted and then easily dismissed. While his relationship with Bianca was permanent, something he truly valued. And if she really loved him, this was one thing she could do for him, leave that relationship undamaged. So winding her arms around her midriff to hold in the pain, she said nothing, staring down at the carpet, her hair falling loosely to hide her face.

'*Why* did you do it? What in hell did you hope to gain by it?' His fury had undergone a metamorphosis to an angry anguish that shook Sorrel's determination to hold her tongue because he sounded as if he was hurting, too.

'It—it was an accident.' The defence was forced out of her.

'An accident!' he derided. 'And just how did you 'accidentally' tell my mother that Bianca is her husband's bastard?' His contempt seemed to strip the skin from her and, as she had no answer that would satisfy him without giving Bianca away, she let him do it to her without protest.

But her silence only seemed to infuriate him further and he seized her, hard hands gripping her chin to force her to face him, uncaring how much he hurt. 'No, don't hide your face in shame, you bitch. Let me see you for what you are.'

Her lashes fluttered upwards, her eyes feasting for the last time on his beloved face. Even in anger and bitter disillusion he could move her, stir the desire to take him into her body to comfort him. Comfort he would no longer accept from her, and the knowledge that never again would she experience that soul-deep fulfilment filled her with despair.

'How you can look like that—like a lost soul who despairs of ever being found . . . I thought what you've thrown away today was something good, but now I'm beginning to think I had a lucky escape.' He forced her chin up higher, his fingers bruising her jaw. 'Maybe your father wasn't to blame after all for disowning you. Maybe you destroyed that relationship, too.'

Sorrel closed her eyes, no longer able to watch the avid eagerness with which he saw his barbs strike home. The bruising fingers tightened still further until she thought she would faint from the pain. 'Defend yourself, damn you!' The anguished demand seemed to be torn from him, 'We had something good, so give me an explanation I can accept.'

Even if she had been prepared to give him the true version of what had happened behind the scenes at the hotel that afternoon, she was incapable of speaking. At last he let her go, and she swayed as the blood rushed back into the veins that had been constricted.

'I don't understand you.' He sounded bewildered, bewildered and defeated, and somehow pleading. Sorrel swallowed hard to moisten her dry tongue but no words would come.

Something dropped on to the carpet at her feet, two keys, one to the building and the other to her door. 'I'll no longer need these, and I think for both our sakes we'd better forget the clause in your contract concerning further designs.'

The clipped words jerked her head up and she watched him walk away, feeling as raw and maimed as if half of her had been cut away without an aneasthetic. 'Luc . . .' Cracked and hoarse, tinny like the voice of a mechanical doll, she couldn't hold back his name.

He turned, his gaze so contemptuous her hand dropped to her side. 'That finally got through to your mercenary little soul, did it? Tell Charlie from me, he got it wrong. There's no little girl lost behind that mask of yours. Whatever it is, it's twisted and ugly.'

The door slammed behind him and she listened to his receding footsteps. After a long time she bent and picked up the keys he had tossed at her feet, then moving like an old woman she went to the door and slid across the bolt. A touch of the switch plunged the apartment into darkness.

Huddled into a foetal ball on the sofa, she knew her brief happiness was over, dying, not from growing boredom and indifference as she had feared, but assassinated by anger and hatred and unjustified contempt, and she was afraid she would never recover from the pain of it.

CHAPTER ELEVEN

THE SUN was shining through the curtains when the doorbell pealed. Still in the same position she had assumed after Luc had left last night, Sorrel ignored it. But a few minutes later it pealed again and was followed by a hammering and Tammy's voice asking if she was all right.

Stiffly Sorrel uncurled herself, staggering because at first she couldn't feel her feet, then shuddering from the pain of pins and needles as the blood started to flow again. Lurching, she made it to the door and after a struggle with numb fingers, unbolted it.

'D'you know what time it is?' Tammy demanded. 'My God!' She did a double-take at Sorrel's transparent pallor. 'You look like hell! Are you ill?'

'Just a bad headache,' Sorrel said warily and with truth. 'I won't be working today.'

'In that case, I'm sorry I disturbed you, only when we hadn't heard any movement . . . ' She hesitated. 'Luc's gone to work, has he?'

'He—he didn't stay last night.' Her jaw still hurt when she talked and in case the bruises might be visible she drew the collar of her bathrobe higher. It hurt even more, though in a different way when she said, 'You may as well know, it—it's over, Luc and me . . . '

'Over!' Tammy eyes popped. 'Oh, come off it. I recognise a besotted man when I see one. You mean you've quarrelled? Well, Charlie and I are always spatting, it doesn't mean anything.'

Sorrel shook her head. Tammy meant well but she didn't think she could bear it. 'It was more than a spat.

171

I shan't be seeing him again,' she said flatly, and when she saw Tammy was about to argue, 'Please, Tam, no platitudes, and I can't talk about it, not yet.' Her voice cracked revealingly. 'Just give me time to get my act together, huh?'

'If you're sure . . . ' Tammy agreed reluctantly, really worried now.

'I'm sure, please . . . ' She managed to get the door closed before the first tears fell. Blindly she crept up the spiral staircase, crawled beneath the duvet and let the floodgates open.

For three days and nights she stayed incarcerated inside her apartment, fending off Tammy's worried sympathy, pretending she was working, but though she sat at her drawing-board, it was only to stare into space, remembering. And if the days were bad, the nights were worse. Long, dark hours when her body burned and writhed for the pleasures it had known, the fulfilment it cried out for. She began to lose weight. From being a slender girl she became positively wraith-like, and Tammy's round face became permanently creased with worry.

'You can't go on like this, Sorrel,' she said at last. 'You'll make yourself ill, and no man's worth that, not even Luc Amory. Don't think I'm prying, pet, but don't you think it would be better to talk about it instead of bottling it up?'

But Sorrel knew she couldn't tell Tammy the full story without betraying Luc's confidence about Bianca's kinship with him. 'Let's just say I loved too well and not at all wisely,' she evaded with a wan smile. But she knew Tammy was right. Twice Bianca and once Hywel had phoned her but she had put them off by telling them she had caught some bug. But hiding away, pining for lost dreams that could never have come to anything anyway was pathetic. Somehow she had to find the courage and the will to get a grip on her life and start again. Not that she could risk seeing Bianca and Hywel, but she could at least stop being such a pain to Tammy and Charlie.

'Nobody died of a broken heart that I know of,' she declared with an attempt at a smile. 'I'll get over it, and for starters, how about you and Charlie joining me for a meal tonight?' At least it would give her something useful to think about, she told herself at Tammy's relieved acceptance.

And the following morning saw her down in her workshop by nine o'clock where a heap of repair work waited for her. For the next two weeks she filled every daylight hour—and most of the night hours, too. When there was nothing requiring her attention in her workshop she went out to haunt the museums on the pretext of looking for new ideas but really to get away from Wapping. For one thing the place seemed imbued with Luc's presence, and for another, Bianca was still trying to reach her on the telephone. So far she had managed to avoid speaking to her, for how could she explain that it would be better for them both if they let their acquaintance drop? Bianca would want to know why, and if Sorrel told her, she would almost certainly want to put it right with Luc. And that was something Sorrel wanted to avoid. Risking Bianca's relationship with Luc wouldn't do anything to mend her own with him. Their affair was over, even if he did learn the truth.

And out of working hours she became an inveterate party-goer, accepting every invitation that came along and staying talking into the small hours because it kept her away from the apartment where the ghost of those all too brief weeks of happiness with Luc lay in wait for her. And all the time, behind all the frantic filling of her days and the frenetic evenings was the hope, the prayer, that she might be pregnant with Luc's child.

The day that Bianca finally caught up with her was also the day when this last hope was dashed. She had woken with the ominous niggle in the small of her back but she tried to ignore it. By mid-morning the familiar cramps in her stomach denied her wishful thinking and she finally had to come to terms with the fact that there would be no child, no compensation for losing the one man she could love.

That was her nadir, when she knew the true meaning of desolation, and her grief was as abandoned as her loving had been, dry, racking sobs shaking her too-slender frame, tearing harshly through her chest, a grief too deep to be softened by tears. She didn't hear when Tammy called to her or feel her touch on her arm. Only when she was gathered to that motherly bosom was she aware that she was no longer alone, and at last her terrible grief was able to find the relief of tears.

Tammy rocked her, crooning wordlessly, her own round cheeks wet with tears of sympathy, but when the storm of weeping was finally over and Sorrel lay inert against her, sympathy turned to anger against the man who was responsible. 'I could kill him!' she said fiercely, 'doing this to you.'

Sorrel managed to sit upright. 'You mustn't blame Luc,' she said drearily. 'Honestly, none of this is his fault.'

'But I thought—I mean, that he must have been in touch with you again to upset you like this.' Tammy was bewildered.

Sorrel shook her head. 'Oh, no. He won't be getting in touch with me again—ever.'

'I wish I knew——' Tammy sighed. 'So what brought all this on? It's more than a fit of the blues.'

'I—I'm not pregnant,' Sorrel explained with a tremulous mouth.

'You're *not* pregnant? Well, most girls would find that something to be thankful for,' Tammy suggested cautiously, not understanding.

'But I wanted to be. I hoped, I *prayed* I would be, so that I'd have something . . . ' Her voice broke revealingly and Tammy's motherly heart ached for her.

Tammy stayed for the rest of the morning, and would

have cancelled an appointment in order to stay longer
had Sorrel not insisted that she was all right now. And
indeed she seemed to have reached a state of numbness,
so that when the telephone rang she answered it auto-
matically.

'Sorrel!' Bianca's voice held a note of triumph. 'At
last I've managed to get you. What on earth are you
and Luc playing at, hiding away from everyone?'

'I—we——' Feeling trapped, Sorrel wondered how
she was going to explain. 'I've been very busy,' she
managed lamely. 'As for Luc . . . ' the crack in her
voice demolished her attempt to sound indifferent. 'I—I
haven't seen him since the night of the launch.'

'You haven't seen——' Bianca began incredulously.
'Then where is he? What's he doing? I've tried to reach
him at the office but he's never there and Peter keeps
saying he's not at the apartment, so I naturally assumed
he was with you.'

'You must know Luc has many other women friends
beside me,' Sorrel managed to say with difficulty.

'Oh, come off it.' Bianca was openly derisive. 'I've
seen him with a lot of lady friends in my time, but he's
never looked at one of them the way he looks at you.'

There was a fraught silence because Sorrel couldn't
think of a thing to say, then Bianca broke it, saying
intuitively, 'Something's happened! Sorrel, has some
bitch made mischief between you?'

'No!' It was the last line of thinking Sorrel wanted
her to take, that some outside influence had split her
and Luc. 'No, no one's made mischief, Bianca. We—it's
just that Luc and I aren't seeing each other any more.'
Her throat ached.

'I don't believe it! He was so—so *happy!* And if
you've just decided to go your separate ways by mutual
agreement, why isn't he talking to me, either? I haven't
even been able to tell him about Hywel and me yet.
There's something more to this than you're telling me,

and I mean to find out what it is. I'm coming round to see you, Sorrel.'

'No!' Panic-stricken, Sorrel cast around for an excuse to divert her, *any* excuse to avoid seeing Bianca face to face. 'I—I've got to leave here inside the hour, a—a potential client in—in Birmingham,' she extemporised. She wished she could say she was emigrating to Australia, and even as the thought formed she realised she had a perfectly legitimate escape route. 'Once that's sorted out I'm going abroad.'

'Abroad!' Bianca sounded stunned and Sorrel rushed on, 'That's right, a jewellery house in New York wants me to design for them and I've—I've accepted.'

'But you're designing for Luc,' Bianca objected. 'You can't just walk out on him. Oh, I don't understand any of this.' There was a pause and she sounded hurt as she said, 'I thought we were friends, Sorrel.'

It was just another hurt to add to the load she was carrying around with her. Sorrel would have loved to have Bianca for a friend. Even more, she would have loved to have her as a sister.

'I'm sorry,' she said over the aching lump in her throat, and because she couldn't bear to prolong this, 'Be happy, Bianca . . . ' She managed to replace the receiver before her voice broke.

After staring into space for some time, Sorrel searched around until she found the business card Seth Dewis had thrust upon her with his offer of work in America. Perhaps that was the answer, a new start in fresh surroundings, where there was nothing to remind her of Luc. Oh, she didn't expect to forget him; in the short time she had known and loved him he had somehow made himself part of the tissues of her body and the cells of her brain. But away from London, away from the apartment where his ghost haunted her, there might come a time when she could remember only the good things, the happiness they had shared, without the hurtful memory of his contempt at their bitter parting.

A little over a week later, Sorrel had it all in hand. Despite both Tammy's and Charlie's worried protests, she had given notice to the landlord that she was vacating her apartment and workshop and her flight to America was booked for the following day. She had so far not actually contacted Seth Dewis, having cautiously decided she would spend some time in New York before finally committing herself to work there. But even if she found New York wasn't for her after all, a return to Wapping was out of the question.

She had spoken to her father who had touchingly showed his regret at her decision, and had telephoned her mother, who had seemed indifferent. The things she wanted to keep—her books and LPs, the two pictures Charlie had painted, her collection of pottery and glass—had been crated and were now in storage until she decided where her new home would be. Tammy and the rest of her friends at the craft centre had been invited to help themselves to any of her other possessions and what remained would be left for the new tenant. Now all she had to see to was her packing.

Dressed in her oldest jeans and an out of shape T-shirt that she intended to leave with the rubbish, she began to empty her dresser. One suitcase was full when her entry-phone buzzed. Wondering who it could be at four o'clock on a Sunday afternoon, she hurried down the spiral staircase to answer it.

'Sorrel?' The disembodied voice was instantly recognisable and Sorrel's heart gave a sickening lurch before starting to hammer against her ribs. She was hearing things, she had to be!

'Sorrel!' As if annoyed by her silence the voice was more urgent. 'It's Luc. Let me in, I have to talk to you.'

Shaking, she leaned against the wall for support, the longing to see him just once more warring against her fear of being hurt again. What new accusation did he want to throw at her? And why now? If only he had left it one more day . . .

'We—we have nothing further to say to each other, Luc,' she managed to get out croakily. 'Please go away.'

'No,' the tinny voice came back uncompromisingly. 'Now be a sensible girl and let me in. I'll only stand here and lean on the buzzer if you don't.'

Her finger hovered on the button that would release the lock, unbearably tempted. But it would solve nothing to see him again. She was beginning, painfully, to get herself together again. Seeing him would only put her back to square one.

'I don't want to see you.' Her voice was high and strained as she fought with herself. 'I can't. Please . . . come back tomorrow.' She replaced the receiver, watching it with a dreadful fascination as her body sagged and slid down the wall until she came to rest in a hunched heap. It buzzed again, like an angry hornet. Once, twice, three times, and then was blessedly silent. And still she stayed huddled on the floor, her arms wound tightly round her bent legs, until the silence lengthened and she let her head droop slowly to rest on her knees.

He had gone. Dully, she dragged herself to her feet and went back to the bedroom to continue with her packing. Refusing to let herself regret sending him away she swept the clothes hanging in her wardrobe on to the bed and began to fold them methodically into the second suitcase. Only when she came to the dress Hywel had made her for the dress show and the clothes she had bought in Luc's company for the pre-publicity did her hands falter. They were going to be reminders of things she would rather forget, yet somehow she couldn't bring herself to leave them behind.

She decided she could put them away when she reached New York, until such time as she could bear to wear them again.

A brisk rap on her front door had her jumping, but when it was followed by Tammy's familiar 'Cooee . . . ' she relaxed, leaning over the gallery to call, 'The door's

on the latch, Tam, come in.' She started down the spiral
staircase as she heard the door open and close. 'I've
nearly finished my packing. Would you ask Charlie if
he'll carry the bags down to the cab for me
tomorrow——' Her words were cut off with a strangled
cry as she turned the last spiral and saw, not Tammy,
but Luc standing in the entrance to her hallway.

Her eyes devoured him; the long, muscular legs and
narrow hips, the broad, powerful shoulders that the
casual denims he was wearing only seemed to empha-
sise, the square chin with its hint of dark stubble, the
strong planes of his face with those slashing lines from
nose to mouth that were surely more deeply etched, the
short, dark hair with its sprinkling of silver, its texture
still remembered by her fingertips, and for those first
few seconds her joy at seeing him flared like a blow-
torch, and seemed momentarily to find a response in
his dark eyes. But of course she had to be mistaken
about that.

She clutched the central newel post to steady herself
as she said tartly, 'Resorting to trickery now, Luc? It
must have been convincing, the tale you spun to Tammy,
for her to let you in here.'

'Yes, she left me in no doubt as to her opinion of
me, and she took some talking round, but I was prepared
to resort to anything short of murder to see you.' His
eyes impaled her.

'Well, now you're here, perhaps you'll tell me what
was so important.'

'His gaze never shifted. 'Aren't you going to ask me
to sit down?'

Already his voice, the force of his personality, was
weaving his special magic about her. Trying to resist it
she said sharply. 'You won't be staying long enough,
and as you can see, I'm busy.'

At last he turned his head to gaze round her denuded
sitting-room, and she was able to move as far as the
one remaining sofa, carefully keeping the bulk of it

between them. 'You're leaving here?' he asked sharply.

'Tomorrow. I'm booked on a flight to New York.' Fascinated, she saw him close his eyes, watched the movement of his throat as he swallowed.

'You're not going anywhere,' he said harshly, his eyes snapping open to stare at her belligerently.

'It's all arranged. Seth Dewis tried to persuade me at the Showing to go over there to design for him, but I turned him down.' She spoke quickly and nervously, trying to counteract the pull of his command. 'Later, it didn't seem such a bad idea after all, and you didn't want to hold me to my contract.'

'And that's why you told me to come back tomorrow, knowing you'd be gone?' He seemed to be labouring under some strong emotion, but whether it was anger or something else she couldn't be sure. She nodded nervously but he made no reply, bowing his head and seeming to contemplate the carpet, so it was a surprise when he suddenly raised it again and shot out, 'You said you didn't want to see me, yet your face when I walked in told a different story.'

'I——' It was Sorrel's turn to hang her head, knowing that those first few shocked seconds had revealed too much of her feelings, and apprehensive of what he might read in her face now. 'I was afraid to see you,' she said in a low voice. 'And who could blame me after what happened the last time?'

'So why didn't you tell me the truth, the last time?' he asked silkily, and her head came up as if he had jerked the strings, her eyes widening in shock.

'Who told you? Bianca?' The question was out before she had time to think, and the flare of triumph in Luc's eyes made her realise how betraying it was.

'I haven't seen Bianca. I've spent most of the time since I walked out of here with my mother.' He began to advance towards her.

Sorrel's grip on the back of the sofa tightened, but she stood her ground. 'How—how is she?'

He shrugged. 'Still shocked. Until today she refused to talk about it, except to ask me if it was true. All I could get out of her was, "She said she was your *sister*—that model, Bianca Fratelli." Well, under the circumstances you must admit it was damning. But today she suddenly asked me, "That nice girl, the one who designed the jewellery, she won't tell anyone, will she? Because she heard, too." It was like a kick in the gut, the first intimation that I'd got it all wrong, so I made her sit down and tell me exactly what had happened.'

He was close now, too close, but Sorrel had left it too late and was incapable of moving. He took her by the shoulders, turning her to face him. 'So why didn't you tell me I was wrong when I accused you, Sorrel?' he asked quietly.

She licked lips that felt as if they were cracking under the tension. 'As I remember, you'd already made up your mind I was guilty. You were so furious I didn't get a chance to open my mouth.'

'At first, perhaps. But as *I* remember it, I later asked—*begged* you to defend yourself, to give me some extenuating circumstances, but you still kept silent.'

He wasn't holding her tightly but his nearness, the warmth of his hands through her thin T-shirt bemused her, making it impossible to think. She slid away from him, moving to the window. 'I—I told you it was an accident,' she said thinly, 'and it was. I didn't know your mother had followed me, and Hywel and Bianca were quarrelling.' She spun round to face him again, adding pleadingly, 'You mustn't blame Bianca, Luc. She might have chosen a better time and place, but you'd told *me* the truth, and . . . and she loves him. They're going to be married.'

Luc let out a long breath. 'So you kept silent to protect Bianca. What I still don't understand is why you thought she *needed* your protection.'

Sorrel looked at him helplessly. 'I knew you'd be

angry with her, that it could have caused a rift between you, even though Bianca would have been horrified if she'd known she'd been overheard.'

'It didn't matter that I was angry with *you*? That it caused the worst kind of rift between *us*?'

She closed her eyes, remembering again his vicious, slashing words. 'She's your sister,' she said dully. 'The relationship is important to both of you. I was merely your mistress, and expendable.'

Astonishingly he looked angry. 'You don't really believe that garbage? My God, do you think that was *all* we shared?'

She took refuge behind her familiar mask of mockery, though there was little amusement and somehow the pain showed through. 'Oh, I know it, Luc. You spelled it out for me and I remember every syllable. "What a fool I was to trust you," you said. "And for what? To gain a few weeks' access to your body!" '

A surge of red stained the skin stretched tightly over his cheekbones. 'I was angry. Damn you, I was *hurting*, and I wanted to lash out and hurt you back. I said a lot of things I didn't mean.'

Oh, he had hurt her all right, she thought, shuddering, and though he might regret his savagery now, he had meant every word.

He moved silently, taking her hands, his touch gentle though he refused to release her when she tried to pull away. 'I think I went a little mad, but I'm sorry, so very sorry for causing you even a moment's pain. Will you forgive me?' As he spoke his fingers caressed the tender skin of her wrist where the pulse pounded and his dark eyes were oddly uncertain.

Hadn't she lived through this fantasy night after night? Luc coming back to her remorseful, repentant, begging her forgiveness? Begging for her love—except he hadn't gone that far. Even so it was very sweet, and with her heart responding to his plea she couldn't deny him absolution. 'I never blamed you for jumping to the conclusions you did,' she said softly, 'so there's nothing to forgive.'

He gave a long sigh, enfolding her in his arms, and it was more than Sorrel could do to withstand the inherent supplication as her own arms crept round his waist. He kissed her temple, his mouth moving on to explore every feature as if relearning them. 'You're more generous than I deserve,' he said against her lips, then his mouth captured them with a gentle tenderness that broke though the armour of her defences more surely than greedy passion could have done.

It was what her heart and soul had craved for through the frantically filled days and the long, lonely nights, and she responded with a hunger that had him groaning and actually trembling against her. His kiss deepened and she clung to him as if he was her last hope of salvation.

'Oh, I've missed this so, my darling. I've hated you, cursed you, *longed* for you all these weeks . . . ' He might have been speaking her own thoughts as he held her in a convulsive grip.

'I know . . . I know . . . ' she responded achingly.

He kissed her again, and this time there was an element of triumph in it. 'So now you can forget this nonsense about flying off to America tomorrow,' he said when he raised his head, and Sorrel tumbled down from her fluffy white cloud.

The bareness of her sitting-room underlined her dilemma as she opened her eyes. 'I—it's too late to change things now. I don't have a home any more. The new tenants take over next week.'

'That doesn't matter.' He swept her objection aside confidently. 'You can move in with me until——' He broke off, frowning, as she began to shake her head.

Until he could find a little love nest to install her in? she wondered. 'No!' She wriggled out of his seducing arms. 'I—it's all arranged. I *have* to go.'

'Why?' The anger and hurt in his harsh demand made

her tremble. 'Why can't you stay with me? A moment
ago——'

'Because I couldn't go through these last few weeks
again,' she said fiercely, the memory of what she had
suffered too sharp to allow her to submit to the temptation he was dangling before her. He frowned and
would have protested but she rushed on, 'I knew from
the start there was no future for us, Luc. You made it
quite clear that a serious commitment to any woman
was to be avoided, and when you told me about your
father I could understand why. You even told me
bluntly you couldn't pretend to be in love with me.'

There was a white ring of tension round his mouth.
'So why did you become my lover if you thought there
was no future in it?' She shrank from the question but
he answered it for her. 'Because you loved me!'

Sorrel flinched, turning away from him. Well, of
course, a man of his experience must have known.
Lifting her chin she said distantly, 'I don't suppose for
one moment I'm the first woman to fall in love with
you, or the first to delude herself that an affair with you
would be worth the pain when you moved on.' Her
hands clenched at her sides as she gazed unseeingly out
of the window. 'Only the pain was worse than anything
I could have imagined. I'm over the worst now, and
only a fool puts her hand into the same fire twice.'

'Oh, you're a fool all right.' He spoke right behind
her, his breath ruffling her hair as his arms slid round
her. She stiffened but he brooked no resistance as he
pulled her back against him. 'And I'm a fool too, for
forgetting how . . . insecure you were—are.'

'Luc . . . please . . . ' she protested achingly as he
began to turn her round, but he put a finger gently over
her lips.

'You've had your say, now let me have mine. The
first record I can set straight is that I never, at any time,
told you I couldn't pretend to be in love with you.'

Sorrel opened her mouth to argue but the pressure of

his fingers close it again. '*You* maintained that I was surely not going to pretend I'd fallen in love with you on sight. I merely replied that I never pretend. Because the fact was I didn't have to. Oh, maybe it wasn't quite at first sight, but by the time that conversation took place, I knew I did indeed love you.'

Sorrel suddenly became very still, as if even to breathe might shatter something very precious. 'You were right about the influence my father's behaviour had on me, though,' he went on. 'I was chary of marriage. With his example before me I was determined to settle for nothing less than the one woman who was the other half of me.'

Sorrel swallowed convulsively. He couldn't be saying what he seemed to be saying, could he? She didn't dare acknowledge that little spark of hope, in case she'd got it wrong.

Seeing those doubts in her expressive face he shook her gently. 'You, you blind, infuriating, *stupid* woman. Just wanted you for your body, indeed! And to put *that* record straight it was your *delectable* body. *You* are the woman who is the other half of me. Surely my lovemaking told you so?'

'I——' His hand still muffled her voice and she lifted it away. 'I know what it was like for me.' She blushed. 'But I couldn't imagine it was any different for you than what you'd experienced with countless women.'

'Oh God!' He closed his eyes as if praying for patience. 'Haven't you understood yet that all those "countless" women I'm supposed to have bedded are a figment of the gossip writers' imaginations? All right, in thirty-six years I haven't lived the life of a monk, but since my salad days the women I've shared a physical relationship with could be counted on the fingers of one hand. They were good relationships and I suppose I hoped with each one that it would develop into something more, something I wouldn't want to let go. But it never did. Whereas with you, my darling, I knew very quickly, certainly as soon as we became lovers, that you were the one woman I wanted to be committed to for the rest of my life.'

That little spark glimmered as her eyes searched his face, finding there only sincerity. But she was still afraid to believe. 'You—you never said . . . all the time we were together you never gave any indication that it was more than just another affair for you. And if you thought I . . . if you really loved me, why didn't you want me to meet your mother?'

He shook his head at her. 'My dearest, darling girl, what do I have to do to convince you I love you quite desperately? In the first place I was under the misguided impression that my actions were speaking louder than words ever could, and I'd hardly have taken out a special licence for a precipitate wedding if I'd only been anticipating an affair, now would I?' Sorrel's breath caught in her throat and that glimmer of hope flared to burn bright and steady as he went on, 'As for not wanting you to meet my mother, I can't imagine what——' his eyes narrowed '—or who gave you that idea. I had every intention of introducing you as soon as I'd got rid of those Japanese buyers. I'd even got a table booked at Le Château for the three of us to have dinner, so she could get to know her prospective daughter-in-law.'

'A special licence! You want to—to marry me?'

'Oh no, I don't believe it? You're not going to find an objection even to that, are you?' The words were despairing but the warm, tender, *loving* expression in his eyes wasn't. It wrapped around her heart, warming it, releasing all the restraints she had put upon it so that it opened up, so that all the love she had so sternly repressed brimmed over into her bloodstream and shone from her eyes.

'Oh no,' she assured him, half crying, 'I'm not going to object. If you love me only *half* as much as I love you . . .'

With a growl he swept her into a rib-crushing embrace

but she made not a squeak of protest, her own arms coiling fiercely round his neck as she pressed against him, wanting only to meld her flesh with his so that they were one.

'*Now* will you phone Seth Dewis and tell him you won't be on that plane, after all?' he said as he lowered her to the ground.

'As a matter of fact . . . ' Her smile flickered up at him with a hint of mischief. 'I hadn't actually told him to expect me. I thought I'd stay for a while in New York to see if I liked it before I contacted him.'

'So you hadn't given up on me.' His hand cupped her cheek and for a few moments his eyes held a terrible anguish. 'When I think how nearly I lost you! Just another few hours . . . '

She covered his hand with hers, nuzzling into his palm. 'Perhaps having so nearly lost each other will make what we have now ever more precious.'

'Oh God, I do love you, Sorrel!; he said in a shaken voice, and beneath her hand she felt his tremble. 'I want to give you the world, snatch down the moon for you.'

'There's nothing I want, only you . . . your love,' she said, then blushing, 'And your children. That was my worst moment, when I knew I wasn't pregnant. I'd hoped I was, you see.'

There was tenderness and understanding as he looked down into her upraised face. 'You can have all the children you want. Our very own family. And a house. We'll keep on my apartment with Peter to look after it for when we have to be in London, but we'll look for a house in the country, somewhere that family of ours can grow, big enough so their grandparents can come and visit, too.'

Sorrel didn't even have to close her eyes to picture it in her imagination. Oh yes, he understood her all right, the craving that was the legacy of her lonely, unwanted childhood.

'But for the present,' Luc went on smiling, 'there's

only one question to decide, and that's where you stay
for the next few days until we can arrange that wedding.
My mother would be delighted to look after you, but
your father might expect to have first call. Then again,
you could come home with me.'

All three alternatives had their own separate appeal,
but Sorrel was in no doubt which she preferred. 'Would
your mother be very shocked if I stayed with you?' she
asked shyly.

His delighted grin told her the whole world could be
shocked and he wouldn't care. 'Let's collect your luggage
and go, then.'

As soon as they opened Sorrel's front door, Tammy
and Charlie popped out of theirs opposite. 'Listening
for screams?' Luc asked sardonically. With one suitcase
in his hand and the other clamped beneath his elbow,
his free arm curved Sorrel against him. 'As you can see,
she's still in one piece and now I'm taking her home.'
He grinned at their startled expression. 'My grateful
thanks for giving me the benefit of the doubt. You'll be
getting an invitation to the wedding just as soon as
we've fixed the date.'

'Wedding!' Tammy squealed. Sorrel found herself
being hugged exuberantly while Luc had to drop the
suitcases as a grinning Charlie pumped his hand. 'I
don't know what went wrong between you two, but I
always did tell you he loved you, now didn't I?' Tammy
demanded.

'Indeed you did.' Sorrel hugged her back. She was
going to miss these two very good friends, but parting
from them now wasn't as traumatic as it would have
been had she still been flying off to America tomorrow,
for now she had a golden future to look forward to.
Luc and his love, not fool's gold after all, but the pure,
unadulterated real thing.

Luc picked up the bags again and held out his hand.
'Come on, my darling, let's go home.'

A TALE OF ILLICIT LOVE

'Defy the Eagle' is a stirring romance set in
Roman Britain at the time of Boadicea's rebellion.
Caddaric is an Iceni warrior loyal to his Queen. The lovely
Jilana is a daughter of Rome and his sworn enemy.
Will their passion survive the hatred of war,
or is the cost too great?
A powerful new novel from Lynn Bartlett.

W✸RLDWIDE

Price: £3.50   Available: August 1987

Available from Boots, Martins, John Menzies, W.H. Smith,
Woolworths and other paperback stockists.

ROMANCE

Next month's romances from Mills & Boon

Each month, you can choose from a world of variety in romance with Mills & Boon. These are the new titles to look out for next month.

NO ESCAPE Daphne Clair
TOUCH ME IN THE MORNING Catherine George
SUBSTITUTE LOVER Penny Jordan
THE WILDER SHORES OF LOVE Madeleine Ker
ECHO OF PASSION Charlotte Lamb
AN IMPOSSIBLE MAN TO LOVE Roberta Leigh
THE DOUBTFUL MARRIAGE Betty Neels
ENTRANCE TO EDEN Sue Peters
WHERE EAGLES SOAR Emily Spenser
PURE TEMPTATION Sara Wood
*****RELUCTANT WIFE** Lindsay Armstrong
*****MAN SHY** Valerie Parv
*****SHADOWS** Vanessa Grant
*****HUSBAND REQUIRED** Debbie Macomber

Buy them from your usual paperback stockist, or write to: Mills & Boon Reader Service, P.O. Box 236, Thornton Rd, Croydon, Surrey CR9 3RU, England. Readers in Southern Africa — write to: Independent Book Services Pty, Postbag X3010, Randburg, 2125, S. Africa.

*These four titles are available from Mills & Boon Reader Service.

Mills & Boon
the rose of romance

Mills & Boon
COMPETITION

How would you like a
year's supply of Mills & Boon Romances
ABSOLUTELY FREE?
Well, you can win them! All you have to do is complete the word
puzzle below and send it into us by <u>30th September 1987.</u>
The first five correct entries picked out of the bag after that date
will each win a year's supply of Mills & Boon Romances (Ten
books every month – worth over £100!) What could be easier?

```
M R E T T E L T W I N M
B I T T E R O O R E H A
N C L H A Y V N E E R R
O I G L R S E E E S O R
S T U O S E S S I K D I
O O H Q F A E R T A O A
R X M T E C N S Y N A G
E E N R N L U D A C I E
A F F A I R R M B R P E
L O M E T E O A L O G W
M O E H A W I S H A O E
R L N M D E S I R E S N
```

Win	Marriage	Kisses	Woman	Mills and Boon
Harlequin	Letter	Fool	Eros	Desires
Romance	Love	Envy	Woe	Realm
Tears	Rose	Rage	Hug	
Bitter	Wish	Exotic	Men	**PLEASE TURN**
Daydream	Hope	Girls	Hero	**OVER FOR**
Affair	Trust	Vow	Heart	**DETAILS**
				ON HOW
				TO ENTER

How to enter

All the words listed overleaf, below the word puzzle, are hidden in the grid. You can find them by reading the letters forwards, backwards, up or down, or diagonally. When you find a word, circle it, or put a line through it. After you have found all the words, the left-over letters will spell a secret message that you can read from left to right, from the top of the puzzle through to the bottom.

Don't forget to fill in your name and address in the space provided and pop this page in an envelope (you don't need a stamp) and post it today. Hurry – competition ends 30th September 1987.

Only one entry per household please.

Mills & Boon Competition, FREEPOST, P.O. Box 236, Croydon, Surrey CR9 9EL.

Secret message _____

Name_____

Address _____

_____

_____

_____ Postcode _____